House On Fire

A Novel By

Arch Oboler

with a new introduction by
CHRISTOPHER CONLON

VALANCOURT BOOKS

House on Fire by Arch Oboler
First published New York: Bartholomew House, 1969
First Valancourt Books edition 2015

Published by Valancourt Books, Richmond, Virginia
http://www.valancourtbooks.com

ISBN 978-1-941147-55-9
Also available as an electronic book.

All Valancourt Books publications are printed on acid free paper that meets all ANSI standards for archival quality paper.

Set in Dante MT 10.5/12.6
Cover by Lorenzo Princi / lorenzoprinci.com

INTRODUCTION

Writer on Fire: Rediscovering Arch Oboler

There was a time, and it wasn't so long ago, that the name "Arch Oboler" was familiar to anybody in America with access to a radio. Along with Orson Welles and Norman Corwin, Oboler was one of the Big Three radio writer/producer/directors who in the 1930s and '40s essentially shaped the new medium's creative and cultural sensibilities. Each man had the highest artistic aspirations for radio drama; each spearheaded innovative, literate shows that made huge impacts on millions of people; each fought with ratings-obsessed networks and sponsors to get quality material on the air; and each left behind a marvelous legacy of timeless programs preserved in archive recordings.

But of the Big Three, only Welles is clearly remembered today – and that has far more to do with his career as a movie star and director of *Citizen Kane* than with his radio work.

Arch Oboler, meanwhile, has vanished from our collective memory.

That's a terrible thing. It's also understandable. The truth is, a culture quickly forgets those artists, no matter how extraordinarily accomplished, who did their best and most characteristic work in art forms that later perished. How many silent-film stars can the average movie fan name today? How many vaudevillians can most theatergoers identify? The forms died, and with them, the names of even their finest practitioners. The Golden Age of Radio has now faded almost completely from living memory, and so the names of many of its greatest talents have simply disappeared – including the name of Arch Oboler.

Born in Chicago in 1907 (some sources incorrectly state 1909) of Jewish Latvian immigrant parents, Oboler distinguished himself early in life as a dynamo of creative energy. When he was all of ten years old he sold a short story he'd written about an "amorous dinosaur" to *The Chicago Daily News*. In 1933 he sold his first radio script, "Futuristics," to NBC; three years and dozens of scripts later he took over Wyllis Cooper's late-night horror anthology *Lights Out*. Though the number of people today with any serious interest in old-time radio is very small, two of Oboler's scripts for this audio *Grand Guignol* have nonetheless gained a kind of indirect immortality. Bill Cosby's album *Wonderfulness*, released in 1966 and still in print, featured the comedian's now legendary routine about listening to Oboler's "Chicken Heart" as a terror-stricken child, and in 1994 the cartoon series *The Simpsons* included a nod to another *Lights Out* classic, "The Dark" – in which a strange fog turns human bodies inside out – in the episode "Treehouse of Terror V."

But horror was only a small part of Oboler's oeuvre. In 1939 the young man became the first writer to have a network radio series, *Arch Oboler's Plays*, devoted exclusively to his work. The scripts occasionally utilized fantasy devices, but for the most part they were mainstream dramas. Major stars routinely appeared on the program – Ingrid Bergman, Katharine Hepburn – and this helped increase the young writer's fame exponentially. Other Oboler series, including *Free World Theater*, *Plays for Americans*, and *Everything for the Boys*, soon followed, cementing Oboler's status as one of radio's preeminent dramatist-visionaries. In 1945 he received the prestigious Peabody Award for Outstanding Entertainment in Drama.

And then it all ended.

Oboler saw it coming. During this period he wrote: "Television will eventually supplant 'blind' broadcasting even as sound pictures did away with silent movies." Throughout the 1940s he positioned himself for this inevitable transition, working his way into motion pictures through a contract with MGM, where he wrote, produced and directed several films with B-movie budgets. Around the time radio drama was breathing its last he left the studio system behind, becoming one of the first true independent filmmakers. Several of Oboler's films are of historical interest. *Bewitched* (1945) is a study of split personality which predates *Psycho* by fifteen years; *Five* (1951) is generally acknowledged as the first post-nuclear-apocalypse film; and *Bwana Devil* (1952) is the movie that kicked off the 1950s 3D craze.

The dynamo that was Arch Oboler never stopped generating energy, and with radio's demise, Oboler never stopped searching for new modes of expression. Though understandably not a fan of the medium, he tried his hand at television with the *Arch Oboler Comedy Theater* in 1949. Nineteen fifty-six saw the Broadway premiere of Oboler's *Night of the Auk*, a science fiction play in blank verse. He continued to experiment with various 3D motion picture systems in several films throughout the 1960s. And in 1969, at age sixty-two, Oboler broke through into yet another new form. He wrote his first and only novel – *House on Fire*.

In its basic plot of two strange, possibly possessed children and their horrifying effect on the adults around them, *House on Fire* at first glance seems to derive from other popular devil-child novels of the era, including Ray Russell's *The Case Against Satan* (1963) and Ira Levin's *Rosemary's Baby* (1967). But despite the spooky goings-on, *House on Fire* is only tangentially a "horror novel" in the generic sense. Oboler is playing for different stakes here, as revealed by the title of the novel itself, which comes from a John Donne sermon: "His mercies hath applied His judgments, and hath shaked the house, this body, with agues and palsies, and set this house on fire with fevers and calentures, and frightened the master of the house, which is my soul, with horrors." Many souls are on fire in this novel, kindled by both apparently supernatural forces (the spirit of a "devil" of a mother dead for the past six months) and ones all too ordinary. As one character puts it, "Suddenly there's the Bomb! Suddenly there's the Hate, black, white, brown, yellow! Suddenly there's the kids and the Drugs – pot, LSD, speed! Suddenly there's Business back to dog-eat-dog, grabbing and swallowing everything in sight! Suddenly it's everybody, running without faith or hope, running, running to the cliff!" Within what appears to be a simple story of possession from beyond the grave, Oboler paints a dark picture of the world around him in the late 1960s – a world portrayed here as unmoored and valueless, in which God has either "died in our time" or else is "running far, far out at the edges of nowhere." It is a black, bitter vision.

And yet *House on Fire* is a richly entertaining novel. It is clearly the work of a radio writer, or at least a script writer; the story is carried largely through dialogue, there is little physical description, and the entire narrative is structured in three parts, like any typical Broadway play or hour-long radio drama. (Indeed, Oboler scripted an hour-long adaptation of the novel in 1980 for the *Mutual Radio Theater*.) Predictably, the dialogue is excellent; the Yiddish-inflected conversations of Sam and Mary Elias may reflect the rhythms of speech Oboler heard from the lips of his Latvian parents when he was a boy. The Los Angeles-area settings are precisely rendered. The story unfolds at a leisurely but engaging pace, and builds to a memorable climax. Thus, both as a straightforward scary story and as a meditation on deeper philosophical questions, *House on Fire* succeeds – and leaves the reader wishing that Oboler, who passed away in 1987, had chosen to write more prose fiction.

Might an Arch Oboler revival be possible today? The work he left behind is compelling – hundreds upon hundreds of radio recordings, a dozen or so films, several books of scripts as well as *House on Fire*. The best of this material stands the test of time. What didn't stand the same test, of course, was radio drama itself; despite various latter-day attempts over the years (including the *Mutual Radio Theater*), the form remains stubbornly dead. Oboler's films might provide a more palatable way in for contemporary audiences, but they are frustratingly inaccessible – low-quality bootlegs can be found, but among his major cinematic works only *Five* has enjoyed a proper DVD release. There has never been a biography.

But this new edition of *House on Fire* gives reason for hope. In its subject matter the novel is, if anything, even more relevant today than it was in 1969. Readers who step into this particular flame-seared house may at times find themselves anxious, even frightened, but in the end they will be rewarded with one of the most powerfully offbeat stories of its era.

House on Fire opens a window for us into both the author's soul and our own. More can hardly be asked of any novel.

CHRISTOPHER CONLON
October 2014

HOUSE ON FIRE

To Jerry and Poofer –
who fear only
unkindness
and
thunder

PART ONE

Chapter 1

The great flame assaulted the sky. In the darkness the red phallic thrust could be seen everywhere, from the sea, to the hills, to the mountains circling the basin that cupped the city. And where the larger mountains shut off the view, the scarlet mirrored off the high night clouds.

And everywhere the people converged upon it; in spite of official pleas on radio and television, thousands upon thousands moved toward the flame and pressed against the police barricades, their faces crimsoned, their ears deafened by the gigantic geyser of flame.

Somewhere among them stood Robin Shepherd. She wept. And the swirling heat dried her tears almost as quickly as they were shed.

The cage slid downward and the Muzak tape sang a muted canticle to Sunday morning.

Mr. Bannerman, 17D, addressed the aged toy poodle alert in the crook of his arm. "He frighten you, Albert? Me, he does not frighten!"

Albert's ears twitched at the explosive snort of Mrs. Cihack, 14A.

"A boy with such eyes!" she said.

"A genius!" Mr. Bannerman said firmly.

"Personally, I don't believe in pushing children too fast! A child should be a child, not a . . . a scientific curiosity!"

Mr. Bannerman said mildly, "To me he appears to be a very normal child."

Again the small dog reacted to a prodigious snort.

"Normal! He rides in the elevator with me, he doesn't open his mouth, his big eyes looking. You could think I was some kind of a specimen!"

3

"To me he talks," Mr. Bannerman told her.

"Is that so? For instance?"

"He says hello, good morning, good evening." At the woman's look: "So what should a small boy talk to an old man? A medical conversation about my high cholesterol?"

Mrs. Cihack's third snort was lost in the opening of the door as relays tripped in response to a tenth floor impulse.

"Good morning, Mrs. Elias," Mr. Bannerman greeted. "We were just talking about you! My heartiest congratulations!"

Mary Elias's face was a Scottish Highlands morning beacon of happiness. "Thank you, Mr. Bannerman."

Mrs. Cihack said swiftly, "You also have my best wishes on your good fortune!"

"Thank you!"

"Such a boy!" marveled Mr. Bannerman. "A five-thousand-dollar scholarship!" He addressed the dog. "Did you hear that, Albert? Five thousand dollars! It says so right in the Sunday paper! Mark Elias – absolutely first in the National Science Scholarship!"

He would have gone on, but Mrs. Cihack interrupted him. "All right, all right, she knows already!"

Mary Elias said, "Yes, we knew about it last night. My husband drove down and got the first edition right at the newspaper." She dimpled. "You know – a father!"

The elevator stopped and the doors parted as a chubby, blonde middle-aged woman entered. As the doors sighed together and the elevator movement began again, she said, "I beg your pardon, aren't you the Mrs. Elias from the tenth floor?"

Mary Elias smiled. "Yes, I am."

"Congratulations! I just read about your boy! It's really wonderful! At his age! Thirteen?"

The proud mother told her that was not until next month.

Mrs. Cihack addressed the ceiling grille. "My Seymour is very artistic. You should see the marvelous picture he made at camp last summer! Pine trees!"

"What college will he be going to, Mrs. Elias?" Mr. Bannerman wanted to know.

"We really don't know. That's two or three years away. He's just a boy."

"But a genius!" Mr. Bannerman said firmly.

"You can certainly say that again!" the blonde woman stated.

The elevator had reached the main floor and the doors were opening. Mr. Bannerman stood aside as the women moved out.

Mrs. Cihack moved away with a parting, "Personally I don't believe in *pushing* a child!"

The blonde woman gave Mary Elias a "too bad about her!" look, then she said, "I suppose you'll be celebrating today."

The happy mother said, "Yes, indeed. Tonight." Her face sobered as she added, "Nothing elaborate. My mother-in-law died only six months ago. But we decided to have a party for the boy's sake so that he wouldn't think we were ignoring the wonderful thing he did." She was looking into her handbag. "Now what did I do with my grocery list?"

The blonde woman pulled at her girdle. "Well, congratulations again. It's a wonderful thing for the whole building!" She moved toward the morning sun beyond the expanse of glass doors.

Mary Elias said, "Thank you very much," as she continued to search through pockets.

Mr. Bannerman's Albert squinted at the green hedges beyond the door and sighed heavily. The old man said, "Maybe you left it in the elevator?"

Mary said, "Yes. Maybe I did."

She moved back toward the shaft and Mr. Bannerman followed her. "And where is the proud papa this beautiful morning?" He held the door as the woman started to search in the enclosure.

"I spent thirty minutes on that list! . . . Oh, he's busy calling up everybody! Honestly, I don't know where it comes from, this science thing with Mark! My husband can't even use a screwdriver, and me, I can't even hold on to a grocery list."

A short, thin-faced man in his late thirties had come up, and Mr. Bannerman said hastily, "I'm just holding the elevator door. She's looking for something."

Mary Elias turned. "Why, Dave! How nice! Mr. Bannerman, I don't think you ever met my brother-in-law. Mr. Bannerman – Dave Elias."

The men exchanged greetings, then Dave Elias said, "What's going on?"

Mary said, "Oh, I was on my way to the grocery and lost the list! Naturally!" She moved out of the elevator. "Somebody might want to use the elevator. Thank you very much for your help, Mr. Bannerman. I'll just have to remember what I need."

"It was my pleasure," the old man said. "Congratulations again! All right, Albert, all right! In a minute! You'll be outside." He put the old dog down and followed the eager, scrabbling feet.

Mary said to her brother-in-law, "Why don't you go right up? I'll be back in a little while. You'll be at the party tonight?"

Dave said, "Yeah, Sam called me earlier. But I wanted to talk to *you*."

"All right, we'll go up – "

"No, no, it'll just take me a minute. I wanted you to know. I came to take the boy to the synagogue."

Mary Elias said nothing. She thought, he's getting thinner. He's beginning to look more and more like that movie actor – what was his name? – Basil Rathbone when he was younger.

Dave Elias said, "I thought about it last night the minute Sam called about the telegram. I said to myself, 'Tomorrow morning that boy's gotta go to *shul!* It's about time he was a little grateful to God!' "

Mary said, "Yes, yes, of course. But – not this morning, Dave, please."

"What's wrong with this morning?" he demanded. "Listen, do you realize that kid is almost ready for confirmation? What does Sam want to do – have him grow up the way we did?"

Mary said quietly, "I think there's a difference."

"Then let the boy go to synagogue once! Just once in his life! *Today!*"

Mary Elias said softly, "Dave, I know how important this is to you but – "

Dave Elias said agitatedly, "To *him!*"

Mary Elias looked nervously toward the elevator. The door had closed some moments before. She said quietly, "Do you think Sam and I haven't talked about it and talked about it?"

"Talking! The boy's almost thirteen!"

Mary said, "What can we do?"

"You're his mother! *Make* him go! If not the synagogue, all right! Take him to your church – Episcopalian or whatever it is!"

Mary Elias said, "Presbyterian. If he were an ordinary boy, I'd agree with you."

"Ordinary, extra-ordinary! What's that got to do with paying your respects to God?"

Mary Elias said quietly, "You've forgotten something. Perhaps a death in the family is more important to children than you realize."

Dave Elias's face lost its truculence. He said almost inaudibly, "All right." He turned away quickly.

"Dave, aren't you going up?"

"I'll be late for the services."

Mary called after him. "I'll see you tonight! Don't be late!" Her hand had gone into her coat pocket. It came out with a crumpled bit of paper and she sighed and straightened it out and saw that it was her grocery list. She decided to wait a moment and give her brother-in-law plenty of time to get to his car and drive off before she herself went out into the smog-browned sunlight. She sighed. What an emotional family she had married into! Was it the ancient Orientalism which made all of them – Dave – Nat – Harriet – yes, even her own Sam – react to life on such a continuously high key? Thank heavens the children took after her own stolid Scottish ancestry! Stolid? Mama's punitive hands, her once-a-year window-rattling fury at Papa's once-a-year intoxication . . .

She smiled at the memory behind the safety of her years, and started forward to go to the grocery to do her party shopping.

"Pie in the Sky," as the newsmen labeled the building, had been a fountainhead of headaches for everyone concerned with it, from architects, to civil engineers, to builders, to rental agents.

But now, suddenly, in the fifth year of its rooting on Wilshire Boulevard, the circular high-rise had caught on, its cylindrical balconied upthrust a landmark, its thirty floors of cooperative apartments completely sold out to solvent Angeleno families.

The one small flaw in the success story was that the hollow, utilities-bearing core of the sky dwelling was still plagued with intermittent service problems; in the "A" quadrant of the tenth-floor circle, Samuel Elias was having his bimonthly workout with the service department of the local Bell subsidiary.

"Look, operator, how long is this going to go on? I'm a patient man, but I've got a lot of calls to make – important calls – I've been waiting over two hours for your serviceman! . . . All right, all right, so it's Sunday – since when are telephones on a six-day week? . . . Hello, hello! There it goes again! I can hardly hear you! Do you hear me? There's the noise! How can I talk to anybody with that noise? . . . What good is a supervisor! A serviceman, that's what I need!"

A melody chimed out of a wall grille, and he said hastily, "Look, I've got to go, there's someone at the door. If it's not him, I'll call you right back."

He returned to the room in a moment trailed by a gangling man whose tool-festooned leather belt was his credentials.

"Yeah, it's a funny roaring noise. Like – like a crowd yelling at a football game." At the side glance the repairman gave him: "Listen for yourself. It's like you hear at the Rose Bowl!"

The repairman put the receiver to his ear. He said, "Maybe you're getting an induction pickup from a neighbor's TV set."

Sam said, "So who's playing football this time of the year? You hear it?"

The repairman said flatly, "Yeah. . . ." He dialed. "Hello, hello, Fred? . . . Yeah! 984-4603 on interference. . . . Hear it? . . . Yeah. . . ."

He hung up and began to dismantle the instrument.

Sam Elias asked anxiously, "Is that going to take long? I've got important calls." He began to pace up and down, slippers sinking deeply into the white nylon tufts of the carpet. "You'll have to excuse me, I'm kind of nervous. You read the paper this morning?"

Tools probed. "Mister, I ain't got time for papers."

Newsprint rattled. "Look! Mark Elias! I'm his father!"

"Yeah? What happened to him?"

"The greatest thing in the world!" Sam grinned. "The National Science Scholarship! First prize! A college scholarship worth five thousand dollars!"

"Hey! That's all right!"

"Sure! He made this electrical gadget, and his school sent it all the way to Washington. Who ever thought – we got a telegram last night from the electrical company – you know, Westinghouse – and this morning in the paper – " His rugged face glistened. "I still can't believe it!"

The screwdriver dove into the instrument again. "So what's five thousand bucks to a corporation like that? Tax deduction."

Sam said, "Yeah, I suppose so. But we're not complaining.

The repairman said, "Jesus, the way they're handin' things to kids! Young punk still in high school can throw a ball, he gets fifty, sixty thousand dollars bonus just to sign up!"

Sam grinned. He said, "Not my kid. He can't hit a barn door."

The repairman wrapped tape around a connection. "A guy works all his life and some smart-ass with a curve ball makes more in half an hour – " He dropped the receiver back into its cradle. "Okay, mister, you're back in business."

As if to corroborate the statement, the internal bell shrilled. Sam hovered anxiously as the other man spoke into the mouthpiece. "Hello, hello? . . . Yeah, just a minute."

Sam Elias grabbed at the proffered phone eagerly. "Hello? . . . Oh, hello, Bert! Wait a minute!" He turned to the repairman. "It's long distance for me." He spoke into the phone again. "Yeah, Bert, sure! It's the telephone repairman. We've been having trouble – "

The repairman reached for the phone. "Let me check, I gotta go."

Sam said, "Bert, wait a minute. He's gotta check it out." He handed over the telephone, and the repairman said, "Hello, you hear me okay? . . . Okay!" He handed the receiver back. "I'm supposed to check into the office, but you go ahead. I'll do it at the next place."

Sam said, "Thanks, fella, I sure appreciate it."

"Send me ten percent of the kid's take!" Tool rattles faded in exit.

Sam laughed, "I'll do that!" He spoke into the telephone. "No, no, I was talking to the telephone man. . . . Well, what do you know! There, too! What do you know! . . . Yeah, yeah, right on page three!" He listened happily and settled back into the leather chair. "Thanks, Bert. . . . Yeah, five thousand. Four years at any college of his choice. . . . Him excited?" He stretched his legs. "Listen, when the telegram came last night, it was like somebody told him it was going to be morning in the morning! I tell you, like ice water! . . . Are you kidding? He's in his room now, making with another experiment. . . . Who knows? He asked me if he and Shirley could use the tape recorder." He grinned. "So who am I to say no to a genius? Hey, listen, Mr. Expense Account, we'd better say goodbye now. . . . You did? . . . No kidding! That's great! . . . Yeah, sure, I'll tell Nat. We were up so late last night I guess he's still sleeping – you know Nat. . . . Yeah, yeah, she's fine. Out shopping. We're having a little party tonight. . . . Are you kidding – ice cream and cake – it's for the kid! . . . Say, Bert, tear it outta the paper and send me a clipping, will ya? I think Mary's gonna start a scrapbook. You know, so the kid'll have it when he grows up. . . . How many gross? . . . Say, that's all right. Nat'll be walkin' on air. . . . Okay, Bert, thanks again for calling. That's great about Macy's! Good-bye."

He hung up the receiver and grinned again. It was great to have old Bert call; Mr. Business First had sounded more excited, when he spoke of reading about Mark in *The New York Times*, than he had been about getting them that Macy's order. Sam decided he'd better get Nat up and tell him about that. After all, they'd never cracked that market before, not even in Papa's time. Yeah, Nat wouldn't mind waking up for *that!*

As he started toward the door, he found himself straining for some sound out of the bedroom down the hall. Mark and his sister had been there since very early morning. . . . Well, the boy genius! He was entitled to privacy for his experiments. Five thousand dollars' worth! As Sam Elias walked, he retied the cord of his robe; after all, there might be strangers in the hall. Not that he was ashamed of his robe – brocade – Mary's birthday present.

Just as he got to the outer door, the telephone rang. He said, "Celebrities!" and moved over to the entry-room telephone and picked it up. "Hello? Hello? . . . Yes, yes, this is Mr. Elias speaking. . . . Oh, yeah, sure, Mr. Dumont, I listen to you on the radio

all the time. It's a pleasure! . . . Oh – well, I dunno – we're going
to have a little party tonight – just for the family. . . . Well, I guess
that'd be all right – my wife isn't here, but just to make a recording – yeah, that'll be okay. . . . Any time after half past six. . . .
You're welcome."

He hung up and sat there. He grinned. He said, "Celebrities!"

The door chimes beckoned. He got to his feet and hurried
toward the entry door. This business of fathering a prize-winner
was getting to be something. He opened the door.

"Good morning, Sam."

Harriet. As always, for a split second he saw his little sister;
then she was the stern-mouthed, familiar stranger of forty plus.

"Come in, come in! Nat still asleep?"

She said, "Yes," and stepped in.

"Come in, come in!" He led her into a curve of the living room
with its far-flung view. A miniature freighter was dissolving into
the gray edge of sea at the horizon.

"Mary here?" She was fitting the inevitable cigarette into the
complicated filter she had recently acquired; he wondered if he
should tell her about that new cancer statistic he had heard on
the radio, but noticing the tense look on her face, he decided
that this wasn't the time.

"No, she's out shopping." He saw the muscle twitch in her
left cheek. What was the crisis now? He deliberately relaxed into
his favorite chair. He made himself smile. "Come on, sit down.
You'll wear out the rug."

His sister sat down on the edge of the sofa. She said, "When
you called about the telegram last night – it was so hard to believe – I couldn't say anything."

Sam said, "Yeah, you were kind of quiet." He grinned. "I
made up for it."

"But when I got back home, I went into my room and I cried
and cried!"

"What the hell was there to cry about?" He grinned again.
"Five thousand dollars?"

"But to us – to *us* – such a thing could happen!"

The amusement drained out of Sam's face. He said sharply,
"Why shouldn't it? Isn't it about time we got a break?"

His sister said, "You got a break when you got Mary."

Sam said solemnly, "Don't I know it!"

"I've often wondered – how you ever got the courage to run off with her – "

Sam said, "That's a helluva question after all these years!" At her flutter: "No, I'll tell you. Don't you know yet it was Mary? Me, I had the guts of a plucked chicken!" His cupped hand slapped his knee. "Hey, come on! This is a day to be happy – full of celebration!"

Harriet Elias was on her feet, moving away. Sam quickly went after her. "What's the matter now?"

"I – I just remembered something I've got to do – I'll be back later – "

"Wait a minute! Wait a minute! You don't run in and out in just a minute! What's the matter?"

"Please, Sam! I – I just wanted to congratulate you about the boy."

Sam looked at her. He said softly, "Harriet . . ."

She looked at the floor. She said, "I – I don't think I can . . ."

"You used to talk to me . . ."

Harriet Elias moved back into the living room. She sat down. Sam seated himself opposite her and waited.

"I've met somebody . . ." she said.

Sam jumped to his feet. "That's great! That's wonderful! Who is he? Hey, bring him over tonight. We'll – "

"No, listen to me! It isn't wonderful! I'm frightened, and I'm miserable, and I don't know what to do!" The face she lifted to him was the one he had known too long – creviced with anxiety.

Sam said, "I – I don't understand. Who is he?"

In the split second before she answered, the telephone rang. When Sam did not move toward the instrument, Harriet said his name and his hand went out and he picked up the receiver. He talked briefly, and when he hung up, he said, "We're celebrities. A reporter. She wants to come over and interview Mark. Before, it was a fellow from some radio station. They'll both be here tonight." He smiled wryly. "Maybe we can get in a plug for Friendly Toys."

Harriet said, "He's an older man."

Sam blinked, then related what she had said to their earlier conversation. "That's okay. More reliable. So where did you meet him?"

"At the office. About a month ago. He's the new buyer for Amalgamated. You weren't in that day."

"What's his name?"

"Max Alt."

He was puzzled. "Max Alt?"

"He took me out to lunch. I found myself laughing like I never thought I could. Such stories – better than you hear on TV!"

Sam said, "That's great. A man with a sense of humor."

"Then I went to dinner with him a couple of times. He likes music, too. He took me to some concerts. I've never had such seats. Downstairs." She smiled. "You know my eyes – for the first time I could see all the instruments."

Sam said, "So everything's going fine. Why are you – "

She interrupted sharply. "He wants me to go away with him next Monday."

"Yeah?"

"For a month – he's driving – Las Vegas – Reno – all the way up to Seattle."

"Vegas – Reno – okay! You can get married there real easy! No waiting!"

She said something so softly that he was not sure that he heard the words correctly. He said, "What did you say?"

"He doesn't want to get married."

"Then the hell with him!"

"No."

"You can't go!"

"Can't?" Harriet said.

"You're not that kind of a person!"

"And what am I?"

"Huh? Why, you're – you're – "

"I'll say it for you! I'm a virgin! A forty-four-year-old virgin!"

Face suddenly hot, Sam said hastily, "So you're a good girl! What's wrong with that?"

"You're goddam wrong, Sam!"

Harriet cursing! Sam Elias stared at her pinched white face.

"Let me remind you of something!" she went on. "Do you remember that time Nat brought home that sweet girl he was crazy about? What was her name? – Ruthie – Ruthie over to meet Pa and us. And Mama wouldn't let them in the downstairs door – she stuck her head out of the window and with the whole neighborhood listening she screamed at them! Do you remember what she screamed, Sam?"

Sam, face taut, did not answer.

His sister went on inexorably. "I'll remind you. She yelled. 'You can't bring that whore in here! You can't bring in that whore!'"

Sam found his voice. "Harriet, what good is this? Why do you look back – "

"I'm trying to tell you! Ruthie wasn't! But I *am!* That whore, Sam! For years! A whore! A whore!"

He jumped to his feet. "Are you outta your mind?"

"I lie by myself in that bed night after night, and in my head men crawl over me, through me – "

"Harriet! For God's sake! The kids – "

She was weeping now. "I want to go with him, Sam! I've *got* to go with him!"

Sam said, "All right, all right. If that's what you want, do it! You're a grown person."

She lifted a wet face to him, and now, to Sam's eyes, she was a small girl. "But I don't know anything! All those years – I didn't want to be a woman . . ."

Sam began walking up and down. He said, "God damn her! God damn her!"

Harriet went after him. She pulled at his arm. "No, Sam! No! Just help me!"

"I – I can't!"

"Sam . . ."

"Mary! Why don't you stay and talk to Mary?"

"Would she . . ."

Sam said hastily, "Sure, Sis! Sure! After the kid's party tonight, you and Mary get together. Okay?"

He touched her cheek awkwardly, and she looked up at him

and she said, "Does everybody live in such a nightmare?"

"That's an old question," Sam told her. . . .

The brown tape snaked around the metal post and a high whistle burbled from behind perforated metal.

The small boy, watching intently, reached out; a relay snapped, magnetic fields seized on metal, and the mechanism came to an instantaneous stop.

At the opposite end of the room, Shirley Elias looked up from Sir Lancelot lancing a three-quarter-page dragon.

"Does it work?" she asked.

"The recorder heads are dirty," her brother told her. "I'll have to clean them."

Carefully putting the book down on the bed, the small girl slid off the chenille spread and hurried over to her brother. He dipped a cotton swab into a plastic bottle.

"It smells funny."

"It's alcohol," the boy told her.

"Like people drink?"

"No. It's a poison, kind of. Causes gastric disturbances."

Shirley nodded sagely. Then she asked, "What's poison?"

"It kills people." The moistened swab rubbed at playback magnets.

Shirley said brightly, "Like Grandma said?"

Mark nodded. He examined the cotton carefully, then remoistened it and began scrubbing the metal once more.

The small girl looked adoringly up at her brother. He is beautiful, she thought, more beautiful than Sir Lancelot on his horse. "Mark . . ."

"Huh?"

"Will you have to go away?"

"Go away where?"

She followed him as he moved to get another angle of the mechanism. "You know! Where you won!"

Mark Elias said firmly, "'Course not. Not for two or three years. It's for college."

Shirley was pleased. "Oh! . . . Maybe you won't have to go ever! If it's like Grandma said."

"Maybe." Her brother's eyes were focused on a fleck of magnetic debris.

The girl giggled.

Mark continued to work on the tape recorder as he asked, "What's funny?"

"Remember that time Grandma had that funny man there?"

"Which funny man?"

"You know. That one from college with the grass all over him."

"Hair!" he corrected her.

"Uh-huh. Wasn't he funny?"

The boy said, "Yes." Screwdriver turned minutely.

Shirley giggled again. "He was funny! . . . Mark . . ."

"Huh?"

"Will we ever have so much fun again?"

The magnetic head changed angle an infinitesimal degree. "Yes."

"When?"

"Soon."

Shirley smiled reminiscently. "He was so funny! Oh, hello, Mama."

Mary Elias walked briskly through the doorway, carefully closing the door behind her. "Well! I got all the shopping done," she said. "I see you're still at it."

"Yes, Mama," Shirley told her.

"Did you work on this all night?" Mary asked her son. "What time did you get to bed?" When he did not answer her, she turned away to the bed and began to straighten the spread. "All right, all right, maybe it's better I shouldn't know. Answer me one thing – why do you have to get this finished right now?"

"I have to," the boy said firmly. Saliva sizzled as he tested soldering-iron heat.

"Have to?" Mary Elias echoed. "Who told you you had to? Did I? Did Papa?"

"No."

"Then don't say you have to." She smiled as she neatly piled comic books. "People will think we're driving you with sticks. So there won't be music at the party tonight. There's always television, God forbid. Oh, I almost forgot." She took a package out of her pocket and walked over and placed it on the table before the boy. "Here. When I was at the store, I got you this so you could flatten that hair of yours down for tonight."

"Thank you, Mama," Mark said. The copper point dipped precisely.

Mary Elias pretended to watch the delicate soldering operation, but her eyes were on the boy. So handsome, she thought. Like my father. But father was a dear fool . . . and this one. . . . She said, "It's a good thing I got it. Your papa just told me that there's a reporter and some radio people coming over tonight." His eyes stayed with the solder flow. "Well! Aren't we celebrities getting blasé!" She opened the hairdressing package. "It says 'Use sparingly.' So you'd better use only a few drops or you'll look like George Raft."

"Who is that, Mama?" Shirley wanted to know.

"He's a late-late movie star with shiny hair." She sat down on the edge of the bed. "Oh, do my feet hurt! I brought back a bundle bigger than you are and they still have to deliver the delicatessen stuff and the soda water." She spoke to Shirley's back. "You know what one of the things was I got for the party?"

"No, Mama."

"Well, it should be a surprise, but I'll tell you. Neapolitan ice cream! When we had parties at our house, that was the big thing. You know – ice cream with layers of vanilla and strawberry and – "

"Chocolate. I know, Mama."

Mary Elias smiled. She got to her feet. "You just wait; someday I'll find out something you don't know!" She shook her head. "I don't know what. Maybe when I visit the moon. Meanwhile, darling, do something for your frustrated old mother, will you? In the kitchen – I brought some more milk – put the cartons in the refrigerator before they spoil."

Shirley said, "Yes, Mama."

Mary Elias called after her, "Put the no-fat milk on the left side." She turned back to her intent son. "On the way to the grocery store I met your Uncle Dave. He's very proud of you."

The small boy continued to work.

Mary Elias smiled. She added, "In case you don't know it, I am, too . . ." She started to put her hand on that black toque of hair; then she stopped, put the hand self-consciously to the side of her own hair and moved tendrils back. "You know something? Uncle Dave has some good ideas. He thought – maybe – " She stopped, sighed. He was such a *busy* little boy. She said inanely, "Can I help you with anything?"

"No, thank you, Mama."

Mary thought, he's so beautiful, and he's always so damned polite! Is that something to be unhappy about? She said quickly, "That father of yours! I left him on the telephone and he's still on the telephone! Sometimes what happens to a child is even more important to his parents than it is to the child." She thought, now why did I say something as simpleminded as that? She began to walk around the room with the pretense of straightening things up. She picked up the new catcher's mitt that had been Sam's Christmas present. "You know, you really ought to start using this."

The boy turned his head, saw what was in her hand, then turned back to the recorder. He said, "Why?"

"Because – well, in a way your father's right – your body's forming new muscles – a growing boy needs exercise." She had a sudden inspiration. "The prize you just won – in a sort of way it insures your intellectual future. So let's start worrying about your physical future, your health, all right?"

"Yes, Mama," the boy said.

His mother thought, oh, why doesn't he ever argue with me? Does he think I'm the child and he's the adult? I *am* tired! She moved closer to him as he bent in concentration over the mechanism. She said, "I – I haven't asked you many questions in your lifetime, have I?"

"No, Mama."

"Well, then I think I'm entitled to this one. Do you miss your grandmother very much? All that time when I was working and I had to leave you with her – you got to like her very much, didn't you? And you miss her very much now, don't you?" As the boy continued working, she sharpened her voice. "Mark, did you hear me?"

"Yes, Mama," he said. He straightened up and carefully put the soldering iron back on its stand.

"Then why don't you answer me?"

"What I'm trying to fix here is very difficult, Mama. And I haven't much time before you'll want me to get dressed."

Mary said determinedly, "I still want an answer."

"I forgot what you asked me, Mama," the boy said mildly.

Mary saw that Shirley had returned. She was standing large-eyed just inside the doorway. "I asked you do you miss your grandmother very much? . . . Well, Mark? It's a simple question. *Do* you miss your grandmother?"

The boy said carefully, "No, Mama. I don't miss Grandma."

"You don't?"

"No, Mama."

Mary felt a rushing sense of relief. "Well! I'd better get busy!" As she moved toward the door, she said to the small girl, "Listen, Madame Curie, you'll have to skip the Nobel prize this year and get dressed. Everybody's coming early."

"Yes, Mama."

"You've got about half an hour."

"All right, Mama."

The moment his mother was gone, Mark Elias made a closing motion and Shirley dutifully shut the door and locked it. She moved back to where her brother was busy once more with the soldering iron.

"Mark," she said.

"Huh?"

"Why did you tell a big fib about Grandma?"

The boy moved the tinned tip along a copper strip. He said, "You know what she told us."

"Oh!"

Mark put the iron down and quickly rethreaded the tape. He said, "Now we'll try it again."

Shirley said eagerly, "All of it?"

Mark tilted the panel back into place, pressed a button, and the tape began to move from reel to reel. "Nope, just the one part."

"Are you going to do the whole thing at the party tonight?" Shirley persisted.

"Uh-huh."

Shirley clapped her hands in delight.

"Okay, now watch the tape."

"I will, I will!"

Mark moved to another table, and the rise and fall of an oscillator note began through the small loudspeaker.

Shirley, eyes intent on the rotating tape reels, said, "Can I ask you one thing?"

"Huh?"

"Can I ask you one thing?"

"Okay."

"Will it really work?" she said. "I mean *really!*"

"Of course!" Mark said firmly. "She said it would."

Chapter 2

Robin Shepherd sat looking out the window. She wondered how she would know when spring came to Southern California. In the midst of all this perennial greenery, how would one distinguish awakening life from the old? She suddenly recalled the small willow she had planted above her parents' graves, and she held herself close in the pain of memory.

The telephone rang on the table by her bed; she got up slowly and picked up the receiver on the fourth ring.

"Hello."

"Hello, there. How's my pretty one?"

"Oh, hello, Mr. Barnet."

"That's not a very enthusiastic tone. How did you do? The boy genius."

"I made an appointment to see him this evening. Half-past six. They're having a family party."

"Great, I'll send a photographer. His name is Farrell."

"Yes, sir."

"Stop sirring me. I'm not exactly Joe Methuselah, you know."

"No, sir – Mr. Barnet."

"What time did you say? Your interview."

"Mr. Elias asked me to be there about six-thirty."

"Good. That means you should be done about eight-thirty. How about meeting me at Scandia at, say, nine? I'll reserve a table."

"Will Mrs. Barnet join us?"

"No, Mrs. Barnet will *not* join us! Must you be so provincial?"

"I am provincial, Mr. Barnet."

"You're exasperating! No, I didn't mean that. You're refreshing. Very! I simply must get to know you better. Away from the office."

"Why, Mr. Barnet?"

Mr. Barnet said, "Jesus! Because me Tarzan, you Jane! It's a date then, at nine!"

Robin Shepherd said, "I'm sorry. I'll be in church at nine."

"Oh, hell!" said Mr. Barnet. He hung up.

Robin replaced the receiver. The handwriting was glowing on the wall. Yes, Miss Buchanan, I'm available again. Oh, I liked the job, it's just that I got a little winded running around the desk. She sighed. Back home, when she had turned down a date, the men had been wounded but retired gracefully. Here they took refusal with fury. Surely there was some way to say no without arousing such antagonism. The fault was hers. She would talk to the Reverend Pauling about that tonight.

Tony Dumont watched the needle exult in the fact that the batteries were fully charged; then he released the button and put the instrument down on the paper jungle of his desk. He reached down, yanked a drawer open, and brought out another tape cassette which he slipped into his pocket with the thought: *that* should cover the boy genius tonight. He looked at his wristwatch. What the hell was he doing? That was hours away.

"Yeah, yeah, yeah!" monitored the speaker on the wall. "She's mine, she's mine, she's mine!"

Tony Dumont reached up and clicked a switch, and the beat of guitar and drums was amputated in mid-phrase.

He turned back to the worn sofa and stretched out. He thought, this station's going to hell with the rest of them. Maybe I should start looking around. . . .

He stretched, yawned. He thought, just in case, maybe I should have the switchboard monster do the wake-up bit. The hell with it! I'm three weeks ahead on programs. If I sleep through the Vunderkind appointment, no sweat. "Mark Elias." The chances are all I'll get out of it is a glass of Manischewitz and a Jewish mama glowing on tape about my-son-the-prize-winner.

He closed his eyes. He thought, to sleep. My specialty.

Sam Elias put the last of the beer cans into the cavern of the massive copper-toned refrigerator. As always, he reached for the old latch on Mama's long-gone icebox; then he remembered and nudged the door closed so that its hidden magnets clutched their opposites in the frame. This kitchen was the only part of the apartment in which he remained a stranger; four months and he still felt uncomfortable amid all of this fluorescent-flooded efficiency of automatic cuttings and washings and heatings and disposals. His mind started down the familiar dark corridor of that other kitchen, and he shivered suddenly. He turned gratefully as Mary rushed into the room.

"Can you imagine that!" she exclaimed. She moved directly to the center table and its burden of platters. "Florence Tengo!"

Sam's eyes adored the humid look of her. He said, "Who the heck is Florence Tengo?"

"I went to school with her! She married a pediatrician in Santa Barbara. It's ten years at least since I heard from her. You should have heard her! As if we were bosom friends."

Sam said flatly, "Fame and friends come to the Eliases."

She turned quickly in time to see *that* look on his face as he pivoted toward the sink. She stood, knife suspended in hand, as he flipped a paper cup out of the wall slot and poured himself a drink. When he turned back to her, she saw it was over. She began to spread mayonnaise on the thin, pre-cut dark slices of bread. She said quietly, "Help spread."

He said, "Okay." He moved over to the opposite side of the island counter and began to work. It became so quiet that each of them began to hear the sub-sounds of the kitchen – motor whirs and air sighs and water burbling in a closed pot.

Sam carefully repositioned a slice of cheese. He said with deliberate brightness, "Do you know what I'm thinking?"

Mary said quietly, "Tell me."

"I'm thinking let's take the kids and go on a real vacation this year." At Mary's startled look: "That's a funny one, isn't it? All those years when you got a vacation, if you even opened your mouth that I should go someplace with you and the kids – well, do I have to tell you? Now all of a sudden listen who's talking about vacations!"

Mary said, "I think it's very nice."

"I figure at last I've earned it. Do you realize this is the biggest month we ever had in the business?"

"Yes. I know."

"I'm going to tell you something. These months since – you know – I look at you sleeping alongside of me and I think, why? Why did you endure it?"

"Endure?" She smiled at him. "I love you."

He moved around the counter to her. He touched her face with fingertips. "The miracle of Mary."

Her arms went around him and they stood close to each other. The door chimes interrupted his searching lips. He said, "I'm gonna tear them out by the roots!"

Mary said, "Those people! You told them not until after six-thirty, didn't you?"

"Sure I did!" He turned away reluctantly. "Don't move!"

"I'm rooted," Mary told him. She turned back to the sandwich spreads. Two pieces of bread later, Sam held the door wide and the buxom blonde of the elevator entered, carrying a napkin-covered plate.

Sam said, "It's – uh – our neighbor."

Mary said, "How nice!"

The woman said, "I'm Mrs. Davis in 5D. You'll forgive me if I'm intruding – " Over their protests she went on: "But after you talked about the party for the boy this morning, I didn't have anything to do, so I made him a little cake."

"That's wonderful! Did you hear that, Sam? She baked a cake."

"That sure is nice of you."

Mrs. Davis flicked the napkin, and the chocolate gleamed darkly.

Sam said, "Hey, chocolate!"

Mary said, "Beautiful!"

"It's just out of one of those ready-mixes," Mrs. Davis disclaimed. "But I know how little boys like chocolate cake."

Sam reached for the icing with a finger and Mary slapped at his hand. "And big boys!"

Mrs. Davis had a hearty laugh. "My husband, too!"

The living-room telephone rang. Mary said wearily, "Sam!" As he left the room, she called after him, "Don't say yes to anything! And bring Mark in to say thank-you."

Mrs. Davis said, "No, no, that's not necessary. . . . They must be keeping you busy. The telephone!"

Mary put the lid on the cake box. "That's a fact! It hasn't stopped ringing! Newspapers – friends – people I haven't heard from since I was a little girl – "

"Well, I won't get in your way – "

"No, no, please stay!"

"If you want me to. Could I help with anything?"

Mary saw the eagerness in the woman's face. She said, "I'd love it!"

"Just tell me what."

"If you'd cut the cheese. No, no, better yet, put the chopped liver on the little crackers on the blue plate. Wait, I'll get you an apron."

"Who needs an apron? Just got to wash my hands." She moved over to the sink. "Where is the boy?"

"Oh, he's got some new kind of experiment going. As usual his sister Shirley is his lab assistant."

"Such wonderful children!"

"Thank you."

"Should I put a cracker on top, or leave them open-faced?"

"Open is fine."

Sam came through the doorway. "Now I've heard everything! It was that crazy Irishman – you know – Joe Regan! He wanted to bring his two kids over – Mark should give them science lessons or something!" He turned to Mrs. Davis. "Did you ever hear such a screwball thing? A twelve-year-old kid wins a prize, so all of a sudden he's a professor!"

Mrs. Davis laughed. She said, "Like my father used to say – human beings!"

Sam said, "Did my wife tell you there's a reporter coming tonight – and a radio man?"

"Sam!"

"Well, what's wrong with that? It's a fact."

"That's wonderful!" Mrs. Davis said.

"I don't know if it's exactly wonderful. Too much of that sort of thing isn't good for the children."

"You can't stop reporters," Sam said. "It's news!"

"Well, it'll still be news if they'd come next week." To Mrs. Davis: "I don't want the boy overstimulated."

Sam snorted. "Overstimulated!" He turned to the other woman. "You should have seen Mr. Overstimulated last night when I got the telegram and read it to him. I was jumping up and down – she was crying – and he just stood there as if I'd just told him that it was raining in Miami!"

Mary Elias said, "That's just it. Everything's inside with him. That's worse than if it were the other way!"

"I told you – he takes after my father, so what?" He addressed Mrs. Davis. "My father was a man that if he was readin' a book, a volcano could explode next door and he wouldn't even lose his place!"

Mary asked, "A volcano in Santa Monica?"

Sam grinned. "You know what I mean!"

Mary suddenly remembered. "Sam, I asked you before to tell Mark to come in to say thank-you for the cake."

"No, no, that isn't necessary!" Mrs. Davis protested.

Sam asked, "What should I do? Break down the door? He's got it locked! He said he's right in the middle of a big experiment!" He turned to Mrs. Davis. "He said to tell you thank you very much and you should please excuse him."

"That's very polite," Mrs. Davis said.

"Oh, that boy!" Mary Elias exclaimed.

"I should have such concentration," Sam told her.

The telephone rang again. "Sam –"

"Yeah! Yeah!" At the door he turned. "You know something – fathers of celebrities have to have good legs!"

Mary turned back to her visitor. "All this must sound crazy to you – "

"What's crazy about a nice family discussion?" Mrs. Davis said. She put the final hors d'oeuvres on the plate. "There now!"

"My, that looks beautiful! As if it were catered!"

"Thank you. Now could I fold the napkins? I have a very nice way so they stand up on the table like little tents."

"Yes, of course. Go right ahead."

Mrs. Davis began to work on the folds of cloth. She said softly, "No, it isn't crazy to me at all."

Mary Elias looked up from her own work, "What did you say?"

"I was thinking about all this happening to your boy. It's wonderful. For me, too." At Mary's puzzled look, "Every time I see your boy in the elevator – so sweet – so polite – I think of my baby. . . ."

"Oh! I didn't know – "

"Oh, it happened so long ago that only in these last few years have I begun to remember again."

Mary Elias said softly, "Was it some sort of sickness?"

Mrs. Davis's eyes were on her busy hands. She said, "In a way. I found out I was pregnant a month after I got married. I wasn't quite seventeen. I threw myself around – who wanted babies? – I tore my husband to pieces until finally he said all right, we'll go to this . . . certain kind of doctor. We went."

"But afterwards – couldn't you – "

"Sometimes if you say no once to God, the no is for always. . . ."

"I'm terribly sorry."

Mrs. Davis's hands hadn't missed a fold. She said, "It was long ago. . . ." She looked at the younger woman. "But today, when I was thinking about my baby, I got to thinking a crazy thing. I – " She shook her head negatively and looked down at the table.

"Please tell me."

"Well, all these years since it happened, I've been very religious. Today, all of a sudden, I got to thinking about all the people who have died since the world began. Millions and millions! I got to thinking – how will I ever find my baby? In heaven – all those millions and millions of people. How will I find one little baby I never even saw?"

Mary Elias heard a faint rising and falling note from Mark's room. She said, "I'm afraid I don't know much about such things."

"I guess nobody knows. . . ."

Sam strode in. "Well, you'd never guess this one! They want him on that late thing! 'Personality.'"

Mary said, "What in the world are you talking about?"

"The television program. Don't worry, I said we'd call them back on Monday."

Mary said, "'Personality'? I never heard –"

Sam said, "Neither have I. He said it just started."

Mrs. Davis said, "I've seen it. It's like a cross-examination."

Mary said, "Oh, fine!" and Sam echoed her unhappy reaction.

Mrs. Davis said, "The announcer sits here, and the guest sits over there, and there's a bright light over him and he has to answer all kinds of very personal questions. I saw that Hollywood actress on it – you know, the one who got all those furs and coats from that general. It was very embarrassing. Like a . . . a confession in public!"

Mary said, "Well, Mr. Elias, that's one telephone number you can tear up! Confessions! That's all he needs!"

Sam grinned. "Oh, he could confess plenty! His big love affair with the fuse box! He's always twiddling with it!"

"Sam! Please go tell the children to get dressed. It's getting late."

Mrs. Davis's eyes followed her neighbor's glance at the wall clock. She said, "My goodness, is that the right time?" She began to unfasten her apron.

Mary said hastily, "Why don't you stay and have dinner with us –"

"No, no, you were absolutely right! This must be just for the family!"

"We'd love to have you!" Sam told her.

Mrs. Davis folded the apron neatly. "No, no, but thank you very much."

"We certainly thank you for the beautiful cake," Mary Elias

told her. She indicated Sam. "It'll be a miracle if there's a piece left for the party."

The older woman smiled happily. "Cakes are made for eating! No, no, I'll find my own way out. You've got so much to do."

The two women looked at each other and suddenly embraced.

"I'm so happy for you and your child," the older woman murmured.

When Sam returned, after ushering Mrs. Davis out, Mary was arranging candy in a cut-glass dish. She said, "That's a wonderful woman."

Sam agreed, "She sure is! Where is she – fourth floor?"

"Fifth. I think she was one of the first ones in the building. Look at the beautiful plate she arranged." She moved to the center table. "Such a tragedy!"

Sam's hand came out of the refrigerator with a beer can. "Huh?"

"She has no children. She told me that when she first got married she – "

A staccato of knocks vibrated the service entrance, the door opened, a beaming fat face looked in, then a large carton entered balanced on a protruding sweat shirt.

Sam said, "Hi, Buddy!" and moved forward to relieve the delivery boy of his burden.

"Hi, Mr. Elias! Hi, Mrs. Elias! I'm sorry I'm late. My uncle Mr. Lieberman, the big brain, he forgets you said rush on the order." He collapsed on the first available chair.

"It's all right, Buddy," Mary Elias said. "As long as you got here. Sam, you'd better put the soda water on ice right away. You know, Nat likes it cold."

Sam said, "Yeah, yeah!" and began to transfer bottles.

Buddy had regained breath. He said, "Hey, how does it feel to be the father of a capitalist with five thousand bucks, huh? Pretty good, huh? I read it in the paper! All that dough! A little squirt like that wins all that dough!" Hastily, to the mother, "When I say such an expression 'little squirt,' I don't mean it derogatory, you un'erstand. It's only when he comes in the store for a Coke, he's

a little squirt; he don't even come up to the top of the counter!
Say, my uncle Mr. Lieberman, he told me to give ya this special
present, you know, in honor of!" He put a pair of small tins on
the table. Mary Elias murmured her thanks. The boy went on:
"Big deal it ain't, just a coupla cans anchovies been sittin' on the
shelf for a coupla years he can't sell. A reg'lar philanthropist, my
uncle."

"Now, Buddy, it was a nice thought," Mary Elias chided.

Buddy grinned. "Any time my uncle puts out, you gotta read
the fine print!"

Sam, still occupied at the refrigerator, asked, "Want a cold
drink, Buddy?"

The fat boy grinned, "No, no, thanks, I'm on a new diet – for
a coupla hours!"

"Who isn't?" Mary Elias said, "Sam, do you have some
change – "

Buddy continued to sit. He said, "No, no, that's all right. I'll
betcha all the television shows'll want the kid, huh?"

Sam said, "Sure, sure, they're lined up!"

"I knew it! What show's he gonna be on, I'll tell everybody."

Mary Elias unwrapped a long salami and prepared to slice it.
"We don't think we want him on TV, Buddy."

"Why not?" Buddy demanded. "Oh! You mean on account
of his grandma! I heard my uncle talkin'! Well, say, what's the
difference – "

"Thank you for delivering the groceries, Buddy," Sam Elias
said crisply. He held out a coin.

"Oh, yeah, sure!" Buddy got to his feet. Fat fingers surrounded
the tip. "Thanks." At the door he turned, "Tell the boy genius for
me the next time he comes in the store, the Coke's on me!"

Sam Elias said, "We sure will." After the door closed, he said,
"Character!"

Mary Elias did not look up from her slicing. She said, "I hope
I've got enough corned beef. . . ."

Sam moved back to the refrigerator, opened it, and began to
survey its contents. "Who's worried about the corned beef? It's
the beer! You know my brother Dave when he gets started!"

"I don't know," said Mary.

Sam helped himself to a pickle. "You don't know what?"

"Stop eating! I don't know if it's right to have beer when the party is in honor of the boy."

"I told Dave we'll have beer, so we've got to have beer!"

"I forgot to tell you. I met him on my way to get groceries."

The pickle paused in mid-flight. "Yeah?"

"He wanted to come up and get Mark and take him to the synagogue." Sam grimaced and she continued, "He said to give thanks to God for such good fortune."

Sam said, shaking his head, "That Dave!"

Mary said quietly, "It wouldn't have been such a bad thing."

"Did I say it would be a bad thing? Listen, when we go on the vacation, I'll talk to Mark." His face was turned from her. "Away from home we'll get to talk. You know."

Mary Elias said, "Yes, dear."

Sam grinned. "You know something – the whole family's excited! Wandering around! Dave – Harriet!"

"Harriet?"

"Yeah, she came up while you were out shopping. She wants to talk to you."

"Something wrong?"

"Naw, she'll tell you." Hastily, to forestall further questioning, "Hey, talking about Dave reminds me! Did I ever tell you the time when he and I crashed this wedding party at the Miramar and we – "

Mary Elias interrupted, "Yes, Sam, you told me. Cut some white bread. What did Harriet want?"

"So why don't you get it cut already?"

"The same question, the same answer. Because cut already it gets dried out." She looked toward the door. "Really, I don't care if that boy is inventing a way to make gold out of bottle caps – go tell them to come out and get dressed. *Now!*"

Sam, sawing on the bread, said, "There's time, there's time. Let 'em experiment."

Mary Elias smiled. She said, "Look who's their new champion all of a sudden! Until last night who was yelling at the boy to go out and play and become another Olympic champion?"

Sam grinned. "So how should I know we had a prizewinner?"

He moved up to her and put his arms around her and pulled her close to him. "Tell me the truth, where did a couple of shnooks like us get such a kid?"

Mary Elias said, "Listen, in my family we've got plenty of bright people! In Glasgow we had a judge and two professors – "

Sam kissed the tip of her ear and moved back to the other side of the counter. He rearranged the position of the bread.

Mary's eyes were intent on the renewed sweep of her knife. She said, "And say what you want about her, your own mother, she was a pretty smart one!"

The smile left Sam Elias's face. He turned and stalked to the sink and began to wash his hands. He tore a paper towel off the wall roller and wiped his hands vigorously. He said loudly, "I felt like a dirty hypocrite!"

Mary Elias stood rigidly. She thought, oh, God, why did I say it?

Sam Elias threw the wadded paper down on the tiles. "Apologizing to Nat, and my sister, and Dave on the telephone this morning because we were having this party so soon after – "

"So what was wrong with that?" Mary demanded. "Just proper respect for the dead."

Sam Elias stalked up to the counter. "For God's sake, don't *you* give me that! Who in the family didn't hate her guts? Name me one! Just one!"

Mary Elias looked at her hands.

"So why do we play games, all of us? Who we trying to kid about Mama?"

"You shouldn't talk like that!" she told him.

" 'You shouldn't talk like that!' " he mocked. "So why shouldn't I talk? What do you want me to do – get ulcers not talking? It's been twisted up inside of me – I'm going to tell you something – I've wanted to say this for six months – I'm going to say it now! When I saw her coffin going into the ground, it was like I started living again! Reborn or something! That's one for the book, huh? My ma dies and I'm reborn!"

"Sam, Sam!"

"No, this time you'll hear me out! Who used to crawl under the house when he was a kid and cry and hide, no one should see him, no one should hear him? What better proof do you want than me? She's six months dead, and I'm working, and I'll stay working! And Dave's stopped drinking whiskey, and you know yourself Harriet's like a new person – dressing up and making like a woman instead of an old bag or something! And my brother Nat, the brains – the time he used to pour in the *Racing Form* and the bookies, now he's putting into the business! He was a nothing! Now he's a man!"

Mary Elias said, "It's really getting very late – I've got to finish here – go tell the children – "

Sam was back at the sink; he quickly washed his hands again and dried them furiously. "And the kids. For the first time since they were born, they're like *our* kids." He turned toward her. "Admit it! Both of them always at her place – day and night – Saturdays – Sundays – who saw them – who knew them? The junk she fed them! Their bellies! Their minds!"

Mary Elias burst forth: "Sam, I can't listen any more! She's gone, so what's the use talking about such things? My father used to say, 'Do only one thing for the dead – forgive!' "

Sam Elias said tightly, "One thing I'll never forgive her for. That terrible thing she said on her death-bed! Never! Never!"

Fine perspiration on Mary Elias' face gleamed; she said wearily, "Please, Sam. Please. Go tell the children to get ready."

Sam hesitated a truculent second; then he turned and went out of the room.

Mary Elias stood there unhappily. An early spring fly settled on the table before her. She looked down at it. Something in the air was different. She suddenly realized that the thin, high, singing note from the boy's room had stopped.

Chapter 3

They stood in the foyer waiting for the elevator.

She looked at him and saw a tall, crag-faced man in his early thirties. He wore slacks, a black turtleneck, and a well-worn corduroy jacket, over one shoulder of which was slung a large battered camera case. She thought idly that he vaguely, very vaguely, resembled Robert Mitchum with overtones of early vintage Walter Huston on the late-lates. She smiled inwardly; what, oh, what, would we do if we didn't have show biz faces with which to do comparisons? God looks like Charlton Heston.

He looked down at her and saw a pretty girl of less than medium height, in a green trench coat, whose face, under long, jet-black hair, was pink and white and who, somehow, looked like an old-fashioned posy. He turned away. This wasn't his year for small, pink-and-white-all-over old-fashioned girls.

He wondered whether she had pressed the elevator button, and she wondered whether he had pressed the button, so they reached out together and touched each other and exchanged apologies just as the elevator door opened.

He followed her into the cage; she reached out for a floor button and he reached out simultaneously, so again they touched hands and this time he laughed, and she smiled, and he said, "I think you'd better tell me where you're going and I'll tell you where I'm going before we require surgery."

He looked at her quick smile and he listened to the soft timbre of her voice as she said, "The Eliases on the tenth floor," and an icicle of memory moved in him.

He touched the tenth-floor indicator, then suddenly realized that was where he was going and he told her so.

Robin glanced at the camera case and said, "Are you Mr. Farrell?"

He said, "No, should I be?"

She said, "I'm sorry, I thought you were the photographer they were sending me."

He touched the case. "It's a tape recorder." Then he added, "I'm Tony Dumont," and the manner in which he said it indicated that he expected her to know who he was.

She recalled the name; she remembered listening to some of his broadcasts, short vignettes of oddball people and events of the megalopolis, done in a vigorous, tongue-in-microphone style. She decided not to give him the ego satisfaction of recognition.

"What's your name?" he said, looking down at her over his shoulder. "You going to do a story on the Boy Wonder?"

Robin told him that she was. She told him her name – Robin Shepherd.

He said, "Who you with?"

She told him and from his "Oh," she knew that he had relegated her to a very low niche on his journalistic scale. All right, so *The Southwestern Weekly* wasn't *The New Yorker*. But it certainly was as important as a local station!

The elevator sighed upward. The Muzak, having rested its ordained moments of silence, began a new tape of Victor Herbert favorites.

Robin turned her head just in time to see that the man was staring down at her with a most peculiar expression, almost as if he disapproved of her.

As her eyes caught his, he turned his head. He said loudly, staring straight ahead, "I hope he doesn't turn out to be one of those precocious little Hebes." At her quick glance he added, "Or a dumb Swede juvenile or a pugnacious Irish brat. I'm full of ethnic clichés."

Robin said nothing. She thought, you look to me like a grownup brat, Mr. What's-your-name. Your suede boots look as if they hadn't been brushed since last season's rain. And that corduroy jacket with the leather elbow patches could use a good dry cleaning. Or, better yet, a hook at the Salvation Army Thrift Store. And that bristle-top haircut! Are you running out of hair, mister?

She suddenly realized he was talking to her. She said, "I beg your pardon?"

He said, "I was just saying there isn't any 'out of the ghetto' angle on this one. His parents have to be in the loot to have a piece of 'Pie in the Sky.'"

She said, "Is that what they call this building?"

He said, "Yeah, I originated it."

Well, goody for you, she thought. And you also originated the words Freeway, Disneyland, and Modesty!

"I did remotes out of this place while they were building it," he said. "It's a cheap imitation of the Bertrand Goldberg twin towers in downtown Chicago."

I know where they are, she thought. I also know the location of the Lincoln Memorial and the Empire State Building.

"They're still having all sorts of mechanical trouble. I hope this damn elevator doesn't stick."

She thought, I hope not. You look like the kind who would commit rape with your tape recorder going.

She felt her face going red so she turned away just as the elevator came to a halt and the doors slid open.

As they stepped out of the elevator, he said, "You know the apartment number? I left the note in my car."

Well, Anthony the Omnipotent he isn't! Aloud she said, "10C."

They moved along the carpeted curving hall. He said, "Each floor's divided into four apartments. The 'C' slice should be to the right."

It was; she kept her hand to her side as he reached for the bell-button. The door opened almost at once and a rugged face peered out; then the door opened widely and they were ushered in by a heavy-featured, smiling man in a tweed jacket who introduced himself as the father of the boy.

Robin Shepherd waited as the radio man introduced himself with that you-know-who-I-am attitude; then she identified herself to Mr. Elias who gave her an appreciative man-look, took her arm, and led her into the living room where he said the family was waiting.

The hallway had been rather dimly lit and the transition into the full brightness of the large, curvilineared room was a little disconcerting; but after she blinked her eyes, Robin focused at once on a small, handsome, dark-haired boy standing hand in hand with an even smaller girl whose blonde hair framed a face for an angel.

"Listen, everybody," said Sam Elias, "It's the people from the magazine and the radio. Let me make the introductions."

Fifteen minutes later Robin sat contentedly on a foam-padded window seat between the two darling children listening as Tony Dumont made his recording.

Before the questioning began, the small boy had asked politely if he might examine the recorder; Robin saw that the broadcaster handed it over warily, but, from the give-and-take of questions and answers it soon became apparent to her that the little fellow knew far more about the tape recorder's mechanism than did its owner.

When the actual questions began, she was fascinated with the poise with which the small boy handled the interview; he was quietly factual about his accomplishment; when Tony Dumont threw a curved question at him, the little prize-winner considered the trick question carefully, then answered, in a manner that avoided the trap, with the aplomb of a seasoned politician.

After a while the broadcaster stopped his angled questions; he began to interview the boy straightforwardly, and Robin decided that even Anthony Dumont's ego had been penetrated by the child's honesty and intelligence.

Suddenly she noted that the broadcaster no longer was attempting to get his own dialogue within the optimum range of the mike; she realized that all he was doing was getting the boy and the rest of the Elias family on tape; in his own time he would undoubtedly edit the sentences as he saw fit and re-record new dialogue for himself to accommodate whatever sardonic story line he had in mind. She wondered if she should warn these people; they appeared to be so innocent, so eager to please, so proud of the wonderful boy. No, there was no evidence to substantiate her suspicions; she decided to remain silent, at least until the session was over.

The man with the microphone had moved over to where the beaming father sat. "No, no, you don't have to get up. Tell me, Mr. Elias, this mechanical genius must run in the family. I suppose you helped your boy with his prize-winning exhibit?"

Robin sensed that the father was torn between candor and human desire to be the image of the helpful father. He cleared his throat. He said, "Well – "

Mary Elias pulled the hand with the microphone toward her face. She said loudly, "No, no, the rules said that the boy had to do it all by himself!"

The microphone thrust itself at the small boy. "Come now, boy, didn't Papa help you even a little?"

Large brown eyes looked up. The boy said quietly, "No, sir."

Mary Elias spoke up loudly again, and the electronic ear swung toward her. "Not that my husband couldn't have helped his son. They are very close."

Robin saw the quickly repressed startled look on the father's face, and she noted also that Tony Dumont had not seen it.

"Fine!" said the broadcaster. He clicked off the mike. "Anybody else in the family he takes after?"

In the seconds of silence which followed Robin heard the rush of traffic far below.

"His grandmother!" Mary Elias had spoken, and all eyes turned to her. "He gets his high energies from his grandmother!"

Tony clicked on the recorder again. "Do you mind repeating that?"

The mother repeated her comment, again much too emphatically, Robin thought.

"Was she your mother or your husband's?" Tony wanted to know.

The children sat cherubically as always, but Robin saw that the adults were tense, eyes locked on the mother.

"My husband's mother." Mary said, again a shade too loudly. "My mother-in-law. A fine woman."

Shirley's small face turned to her brother. She smiled and nodded her head.

Love of grandmother, thought Robin. How nice. She suddenly remembered her own grandmother – pioneering matriarch – the weather-flogged farm house – the ice-cold glasses of cellar-made root beer and the smell of rising bread. . . .

Tony Dumont and his microphone were before the heavy-bellied older brother, "And you, sir?"

Harriet Elias nudged him. "Nat!"

"Huh?" The heavy, florid-faced man returned from his inner trip.

"Your relationship to the boy? For the record."

"I – I'm the oldest uncle. Nat L. Elias. I'll give you my card." He fumbled at his pocket and held out a card. "The Friendly Toy Corporation. It was founded by my father. He is deceased."

Dave Elias spoke up for the first time since he had mumbled greetings. Beer sloshed as he waved his glass. "Friendly Toys, Incorporated! Tell 'em about your new friendly line – the friendly atomic rockets – "

Nat Elias forced a grin. He said, "Will you listen to him! One celery tonic and he's a comic on television!"

Sam said, "My brother Dave was also with the toy company until a few months ago. Now he's attending U.C.L.A. to get his degree."

Dave Elias said, "Rah, rah, rah!"

"What's there to be ashamed of?" Sam demanded. "Lotsa people never finish school and go back later."

Tony Dumont thrust the microphone at Harriet Elias. She pulled back as if from a reptile.

"And you are – " the broadcaster prompted.

She blinked. She said, "I am Aunt Harriet."

"Married name?"

"*Miss* Elias," Harriet told him.

The broadcaster looked down at her intently. He said, "I've met you before, haven't I?"

"No – I don't think so."

"Harriet Elias . . . Harriet Elias . . . somehow that rings a bell somewhere."

Again Robin Shepherd felt tension in the room, saw it in the stiffened backs, the fixed looks of everyone in the family.

She felt a small hand on her arm and she looked down and saw that little Shirley was caressing the soft nap of her sleeve. She smiled down and got that wonderful smile in return; when she looked up she saw that Tony Dumont was intent on the job of changing tapes.

Mary Elias began to press refreshments on her visitors; chimes rang and Sam went to the door to return with a neatly-dressed blond young man with a Rolleiflex in hand who looked like an undergraduate candidate for handsomest man on the campus. He introduced himself as the photographer for whom Robin had been waiting.

"The traffic on the San Diego Freeway was fantastic," he told them after individual introductions by Sam Elias. "I could have climbed out of my car and made better time running over the rooftops."

This led to the usual general discussion of the perils of the L.A. autostrades and remembrances of fender bends past and present. Robin caught a glimpse of Tony Dumont, recorder case on shoulder, giving her a good-bye salute in the doorway. And with that gesture, again that disconcerting look she had seen in the elevator; even as she puzzled, he turned and was gone.

Robin turned back to her purpose for being there; she told the photographer to take his pictures as he pleased, then she turned to the small ones. She said, "Tired?"

Shirley's angelic face glowed. She said, "Oh, no, Miss Shepherd!"

She even remembers my name! What a child, Robin thought.

Sam Elias said, "How about you, Mark? Worn out from your broadcasting?"

Uncle Nat said, "Sure he's tired! Look at the time!"

Sam said, "He stays up all night sometimes!"

Uncle Nat said, "Oh, fine, is this something to tell strangers? A boy his age!"

Sam grinned, "So what is he doing, nightclubbing? It's his experiments!"

Mary Elias said, "We're holding up Miss Shepherd. Mark, are you tired?"

"No, Mama," he said.

Sam said, "There you are! All that fuss!"

Uncle Nat said, "So what was I doing, committing some kind of a crime? I was only thinking of the boy's welfare."

Robin saw what the others had not been seeing – that her blond photographer had been busily snapping candids. She did not quite know how those pictures of inter-family argument would fit into her story, but at least the photographs would be available. Including some candids of that younger uncle – Dave, they had called him – who burbled in sleep on a far corner of the great, curved, built-in sofa.

She began to question the children in areas that the radio man had not covered, from Mark's attitude about school to Shirley's role as his lab assistant.

The blond Mr. Farrell suddenly materialized from behind a chair; he said to Robin, "Don't you think we should have a photograph of the boy in his laboratory?"

The proud father said, "That's in his bedroom. Go ahead."

Mark Elias said firmly, "No, Papa."

Sam Elias said, "Huh? Why not?"

Mary Elias said, "Because it's a mess."

Uncle Nat said, "What's he got in there? A secret weapon he's working on for the War Department?"

Robin Shepherd said, "It's your decision, Mark. Of course we'll abide by it."

The photographer shrugged his shoulders and moved away.

Robin had a thought; she said to the boy, "Could you possibly bring a piece of your apparatus out here so we could photograph it?"

His father said, "Sure, why not? Hey, how about the tape recorder you've been working on all day?"

Uncle Nat muttered, "Can you imagine! Twelve years old and he's already classified."

Mark said, "Yes, Papa." He moved toward the door and Shirley started after him.

Sam Elias said, "Hey, do you need any help?"

"No, Papa."

Mary Elias caught her small daughter by her trailing dress. "And where do you think you're going?"

Shirley dimpled. "To help."

Her mother said, "All right," and released her. Shirley skipped quickly after her brother.

Mary Elias smiled at Robin. "She's always got to help."

Sam Elias said, "Listen, where else could he get such expert help at minimum wages?"

"She's such a sweet little girl," Harriet told Robin.

"She is, indeed," Robin agreed. She thought, she could be our child. Howard's and mine. She turned and began to look out the window at the neons, like frozen fireworks, far below.

In a surprisingly few moments the children were back, the boy carrying what was apparently a tape recorder while the girl staggered under a small, enclosed loudspeaker.

Sam Elias jumped up to help and in a few moments the apparatus was set up on an end-table, Mark was posed in front of it, and the blond photographer was leaping around with his Rollei.

As she watched the children, Robin felt a warm rush of air. She looked up. Heating on a day like this? She looked at the others; they all seemed quite comfortable. Again she felt the rush of warmth. Ill? What day was this? No, no, that wasn't due yet for a day or two. And the Visitor would have meant the usual headache, a few hours weariness, not this, this strange, feverish sensation.

Warmer and warmer – she could feel the wet of perspiration on her forehead. She looked at the others; no one appeared to be perspiring; they were watching proudly as the boy stood before the camera.

With the growing heat, Robin had another sensation, the strangest she'd had in all her life. All at once it was as if the lights in the room were going down, bit by bit. And, as they dimmed, they were turning red, a dark red, like dried blood. Robin shivered. She wondered if she was going to faint. Should she lower her head? No, the people all around – too ridiculous!

Yet it was growing darker in the warmth, and the room was suddenly old, very old, an aged room in an ancient place. . . .

She couldn't sit any longer; she got up and walked to the window and stood there as if it were the view that had brought her to her feet. The red dark went away quickly but the heat remained; she longed to press her forehead against the cool of the glass; didn't anyone there but her realize how hot it had become?

A whisper: "You feel it, don't you?" Harriet Elias had moved silently up alongside of her.

Robin did not quite know what to say. She looked at the older woman.

"You are a sensitive," Harriet whispered. "You and I must meet and talk. Soon."

Sensitive? Sensitive to what? Was she talking of this warmth, this strange heat, this stupidity of furnace heat on a warm spring night?

"You better come away, they'll notice," Harriet said. She

raised her voice: "Yes, yes, it's a marvelous sight. Like from a mountaintop."

It was suddenly unbearable. Robin said loudly, "I'm sorry. I must go." At the startled looks, she added quickly, "I have enough material. Thank you so very much."

Mary Elias protested, "But you haven't eaten a thing! At least a little piece of cake!"

"Sure, come on; if you're through working at least stay and hear Mark's new invention," Sam Elias told her.

"A tape recorder an invention?" snorted Uncle Nat.

"Listen, if he says it's an invention, it's an invention!" defended the father.

Robin thought, don't they see how hot I am, how I'm dripping with sweat? She managed to say something intelligible about deadlines, endured a round of handshakes – what a firm, manly shake the boy had! – she accepted the sweet kiss Shirley gave her, and in a few moments she was out of the apartment, the photographer trailing her.

In the descending elevator, Bob Farrell said, "Are you ill?"

The heat was gone now. As if it had never been. She said, "No, not at all." She looked at him. "Was it very warm in that room?"

She saw he was quite perplexed. He said, "No. If anything it was too cold. Are you sure you're all right?"

She said sharply, "Yes, yes, of course I am!" Then, as always, she was quickly contrite. She said, "Sorry. It's been a long day."

She saw that he had small laugh crinkles at the corners of his eyes when he smiled. He said, "I wouldn't know that. You look like my mother's rose garden at dawn."

She was startled. Men, at least the ones she had met in the past year, didn't talk like that. . . . He was, indeed, a very handsome man. But with no indices of the arrogance she had found in other pretty men. No, it was unfair to call him pretty, she decided. It was an aesthetic face, yes, a poet's face. A very satisfactory face. Male. What a stupid thought!

The elevator continued its descent; she liked the way Bob Farrell respected her weariness and did not try to make further conversation.

He matched his steps to hers as they moved out of the elevator towards the exit. He said, "Mr. Dumont didn't appear to be very happy when he left."

She said, "Why do you say that?"

"The story wasn't sensational enough for him. Now if the boy had confessed that he really hadn't made that scientific gizmo, that he'd cheated, that his father had made it for him! Have you heard Mr. Dumont's pitch on the air?"

Robin told him yes, she had.

"Then you know. Blood on the freeways – a suicide teetering on a hotel ledge – a politician pleading that his claw wasn't in the till – that's Mr. Dumont's cup of tea. Nerve-end, high-tension stuff."

Robin asked, "What will he do about this story?"

The photographer said, "I doubt if he'll use it. It's all too ordinary."

Robin shivered. She looked up at the sky. A million cold stars stared distantly. She thought, please don't go away, Mr. Farrell. Stay and talk to me. About ordinary things . . .

Bob Farrell said, "You in a hurry?"

She looked at him. She shook her head negatively. The Reverend Pauling would be there the next night or the next.

He said, "Great! Let's take my car. There's a Wil Wright's right up the Strip."

In the Elias apartment the children had left the living room; the five adults sat in silence. Dave Elias had just awakened; he looked at each tense face in turn.

Harriet said, "They never forget, do they?"

Dave grimaced; he reached for another beer bottle.

Sam said, "What difference does it make? The story's going to be about the boy, that's all!"

Nat Elias shifted his weight. "That's right!"

"And what else will it say?" Harriet asked them softly.

Mary Elias spoke up brightly, "Come on, everybody! What's the use of a buffet if nobody eats? Dave, how about a nice corned beef sandwich?"

The youngest Elias brother shook his head. Beer foamed in his glass.

Mary said, "Nat?"

Nat Elias said, "Okay." He speared a meat cut off the plate she held out to him. He sighed deeply as if to expel some of his unhappiness. "You know, all these prizes for science and improvements and all that – I tell ya one thing's not like it used to be – corned beef! Remember those corned beef sandwiches we used to get down at old what's-his-name? – you know – around the corner from that place that sold milk and cheese – "

Sam said, "Mafolski's." He singsonged, "Old Man Mafolski, finger on his scale-ski!"

Even Harriet managed a smile at that old memory. Nat said, "Yeah, Mafolski's! Now that was corned beef! One sandwich – a regular meal!"

"And the mustard!" Sam reminded him. "It jumped at you outta the jar!"

Harriet said, "I think this corned beef is very nice. I do."

Mary said, "Thank you, Harriet, but for what comes out of a delicatessen, I don't take bows or boos from the gallery." She picked up an empty plate. "I'll get some more pickles."

Nat held up a piece of corned beef. "Look at it! Fat – all fat – thin like paper – " He popped it into his mouth and chewed sadly.

Dave waved his glass. "That's what I like about you, Nat. You're a man of principle. You don't like the corned beef, you don't eat it!"

"Very funny!" Nat managed through his mouthful.

Sam laughed, then called toward the kitchen, "Mary! When you come in, bring some more bagels, please!" He turned to his older brother. "Great news about that Macy's order, huh?"

Nat Elias nodded his heavy gray-thatched head. "Yeah. They still can't beat Papa's invention, those Japs."

Dave Elias had wandered back from a sideboard, a beaded beer bottle in hand. He said thickly, "They'll find a way! They've got energy and ingenuity."

Nat Elias snorted. "Listen to him! The economics genius! But to stay in the business he can't! A college boy all of a sudden! Thirty-five years old! He said it himself – rah-rah!"

"So where's the skin off your nose?" Dave demanded. "It's outta my share!"

"Sure, sure, me it doesn't affect!" his brother told him. "The business is now all automatic – human beings I don't need – everything makes itself, wraps itself, sells itself – "

Mary Elias entered, bearing pickles and a plate piled high with bagels. "Did somebody ask for bagels?"

Harriet rose. "Let me help you."

"Thank you."

Sam's forefinger and thumb captured a pickle. He said, "The other day I heard a joke about a bagel."

"Go ahead! We could use a joke," Nat told him.

"Okay. The joke is: What is a bagel? A bagel is a Jewish dough-nut with hardening of the arteries!" At Nat's groan: "So what's the matter? It's anti-Semitic or something?"

"It was very funny," Mary reassured him.

"Yes, it was," said Harriet.

She had expected his car to be a small, economical Beetle in key with his free-lance photography; instead it was a low, late Detroit model with one of those animal names she could never remember. She realized he must have seen her startled look, because as soon as they had pulled out into traffic, he told her that all his life he had owned automotive junk; recently, after selling one of his photographs to a major magazine, he had made the leap into this, his first sound-fendered, nonstalling piece of trans-portation.

She liked the open manner in which he confessed his admit-tedly immature want of a flashy car; she was weary of the end-less rationalizations people used to justify self-indulgences.

In her year in Los Angeles Robin had never been in the special conceit of one of the Wright ice-cream parlors; she was delighted with the nostalgia of the brass chairs, the marble-topped tables, the bare light bulbs gleaming through the varicolored candy jars. Above all, she liked the brightness; somehow she wanted light, pouring light. She told Bob (they were quickly on a Robin-Bob basis) that it was just like the ice-cream parlor that they used to have at home. He wanted to know where home was, and she told him that she was certain he had never heard of it – Mercoe, Minnesota.

The menu was so huge that she gratefully accepted his suggestion of a hot fudge sundae. After the waitress had gone with the order, Bob asked Robin how large Mercoe was, and she told him that the population, when she had left, was exactly six hundred, not including Mrs. Schmeckpepper's pregnancy.

He did not quite believe that Schmeckpepper, but she swore to the authenticity of the name, as well as the Grautmans, the Hebeisens, and the Klanckes, who had pioneered the small community.

In turn he told her about the polyglot Chicago neighborhood in which he had spent his youth; she enjoyed the fact that he spoke without the self-conscious attempts at clever turns of phrase, without all the punnery and cuteness that she had found passed for conversation in the local newspaper-magazine world she had known for the past year.

Under his questioning, she told more about herself; he was so easy to talk to; she listened to herself in wonder as she gushed on, down to the detail that she had played flute in the high school marching band.

"A harpist, yes," he told her. "A flutist, never!"

The hot fudges came – a mountain of peppermint ice cream glaciered with chocolate. Between mouthfuls she told him about the University of Minnesota, the accidental death of her parents, the small trust fund that had enabled her to finish her journalism courses, then the job on a St. Paul newspaper.

As she talked on, she found herself thinking, hey, Miss Shepherd, watch it, it's been so long since you've sat and talked to someone really around your own age, someone whose eyes weren't undressing you garment by garment, that you're talking the way Mother used to say – with your tongue and your brain unhinged!

She stopped speaking with the excuse that her hot fudge was cooling off; as she ate, he began to tell of himself – his youth in Chicago – the self-consuming actress mother – the business-dedicated father – his own lifelong interest in the filmed image. She spooned ice cream and enjoyed the deep texture of his voice, the lightning darts of emotion on his elegant face. Until he spoke of Vietnam. The word, and the look of him, triggered open tightly shut memory cells; the floor tilted and the chandelier began to spin slowly. She fumbled for the water glass; she heard his quick, concerned inquiry; the cold water steadied her and she told him it was her fatigue, could they please go.

He drove her back to her car, and with a final admonishment to get some rest, stood waiting until she was safely into the stream of traffic.

As Robin drove off, she told herself firmly that she had been a fool to react so emotionally all that evening. First the stupidity at the Elias's apartment, and then falling apart at the ice-cream parlor. Her concentration, as always, must be in the here and now. Oh, Howard, dear Howard!

Chapter 4

Sam said, "Stop being so impatient! They're picking out a nice tape to play us. So it'll take a few minutes! They've been working on it all day!"

Nat mumbled, "What's to work on a tape recorder?"

"Don't they ever eat anything?" Harriet asked. "They hardly touched their plates."

Sam grinned. "Too excited, I guess."

"They've never been heavy eaters," Mary said, "either one of them."

"They're such well-behaved children." Harriet smiled.

"Thank God for that!" Uncle Nat muttered.

Dave Elias looked at Mary. He said, "That's what I want them to do. Isn't that right, Mary?"

Mary said quietly, "Yes, Dave."

"Yes, Dave, what?" Nat demanded.

"Dave wants to take the children – Mark – to church – synagogue," Mary told him.

Sam said, "Sure, it's a good idea. We're working on it. Honest, Dave."

Nat Elias turned toward his younger brother. He said, "When will you learn to mind your own business?"

Dave said harshly, "It *is* my business! And yours! Isn't it about time this whole family got down on its knees and thanked God? *Isn't it?*"

His older brother looked at him steadily. He said, "I think it's about time you stopped drinking beer. It doesn't go with your new image of conscience for the family." He turned to Sam. "Tell me something. What college is the scholarship for?"

"Any one at all, I guess." He grinned. "Harvard – Yale – Princeton – "

"And what's wrong with U.C.L.A.?" Dave demanded.

"Take it easy, student," Sam grinned. To Nat: "Who knows what college? Plenty of time to decide."

"That's what I'm getting at!" Nat told him. "Do you get the scholarship money to hold right away, or do they hold it?"

"I don't know."

"That's what you gotta find out! If you get it now, you could invest it until it comes time for the kid to use it."

"But how do you invest a scholarship?" Mary asked. "It's not cash."

"Make 'em *give* you cash! They've got no right to hold on to the kid's assets for two, three, four years. He won, so it's his!"

Sam shook his head. "What's this all of a sudden?"

Nat said, "I've been thinking about it ever since it happened. All this publicity – the newspapers – I think it's better if you get the money now, put it away before, you know, they change their minds."

Mary Elias looked at him unbelievingly. "Change their minds? Why should they do that?"

In the tense silence Harriet spoke in a whisper. "Things could come out. . . ."

Mary said, "That's ridiculous! What has Mark got to do with – " Her hands fluttered. "He's a child!"

The door chimes sounded; she started to get to her feet, but Sam stopped her. "I'll go."

After her husband had left the room, Mary Elias looked at her relatives. She said, "When will you people learn that yesterday isn't today?"

No one answered her; in the hall beyond a door sounded, then voices. Sam returned, ushering in the gaunt Mrs. Cihack of the morning's elevator episode. With the woman was an anemic-looking, blue-denimed teen-ager.

"I'm Mrs. Cihack, dear!" the woman said vigorously. "I just had to – oh, you have company!" As the men started to rise, she gushed on, "Don't bother getting up, I should have remembered your little family gathering. I know it's late, but we're only going to take a second, my son Seymour and I. Where is the party boy?"

"He's getting something in his room," Mary Elias said. "It's nice to see you again." She began to introduce the others.

Greetings over, Mrs. Cihack settled herself comfortably as the boy hovered near her. "Well, I've only got a minute. When I came back this morning and Seymour heard me tell my husband about your son's good luck, this dear, sweet boy of mine simply insisted that I bring him down here to make this little gesture of his happiness at Mark's good fortune. Show them, Seymour! Don't be shy! Show them the package!"

Seymour sullenly held up a thin, tissue-wrapped rectangle.

"That's very thoughtful of you," Mary said. "Sam, go get the children. I know Mark will be very appreciative."

Mrs. Cihack's eyes inventoried the tabletop. "My goodness, aren't those the cutest little sandwiches! Where did you get them catered?"

Mary said, "Please forgive me. I don't know where my head is tonight. Won't you have something?"

"No, I really couldn't!" Mrs. Cihack protested. She began to heap a plate. "Maybe just a snitch. All those beautiful things! Sit down, Seymour, sit down!"

Seymour's voice matched the look on his face. "Aw, come on, Ma! You promised!"

"Such vitality, always impatient," explained Mrs. Cihack. She bit into a sandwich. "Have a banana."

Mary held out the fruit bowl. "Yes, have something, Seymour."

The adults watched wide-eyed as the boy removed the enormous bunch of grapes that had been the centerpiece of the plate.

"Is that fruit washed?" Mrs. Cihack asked.

Mary reassured the mother; she invited the boy to sit down.

"No, we gotta go. In a minute," Seymour stated through a prodigious mouthful of grapes.

Mrs. Cihack was now lavishing chopped liver on a piece of rye. "He's got all the temperament of a true artist! Oh, here's the prize-winner!"

Sam, trailed by the children, had come into the room.

"Seymour, give him the present! Give him the present!"

Seymour thrust the package at Mark.

"Thank you," said Mark.

"Well, open it, open it!" Mrs. Cihack demanded. "Wait'll you see it! You'll die!"

"I should hope not," Sam grinned. "Go ahead, Mark."

"I'm counting up to twenty-five," Seymour stated darkly.

"He's so vital!" said his mother. "But very gifted. You'll see."

Mark tore away the tissue paper; the others clustered around.

"It's one of the paintings he made last summer at the camp," Mrs. Cihack stated. "I told you – very gifted."

Mary Elias said quickly, "It's – it's very nice. Isn't it, Sam?"

Sam managed a "Yeah."

In the ensuing silence, Nat found voice. "It's – it's certainly a picture!"

"How very nice!" Harriet said.

Mrs. Cihack swallowed a morsel and focused on Dave Elias, who was still staring at the canvas.

"Mr. Elias – Dave, isn't it? – I never forget a name once I hear it – I haven't heard your opinion of my son's work. Now don't be shy! Speak up! An honest opinion is an honest opinion."

Dave Elias weaved slightly. "Madam," he said, "as you know, the artist Van Gogh cut off his ear. I suggest that in your son's case you immediately cut off more, much more!" He bowed deeply and reseated himself, glass still in hand.

Mrs. Cihack rose to her feet, her face flushed with quick indignation. "Well! Seymour! We must go!"

Mary and Sam Elias converged on her. "I'm sorry – he hasn't been feeling well – " "Too many beers – pay no attention – "

Mrs. Cihack was already at flank speed toward the door. "I understand – it's perfectly all right – why dignify ignorance with remarks such as I now could make!"

"Thank you ever so much for the lovely present! Believe me!" Mary called at the closing door.

Sam took the picture from his son. He looked at it with changing angles. He said, "I give up."

Mary said sadly, "Dave, Dave!"

Nat Elias said, "For once I must agree with him!"

Harriet said, "I think it was a very nice thought, giving a picture."

"It certainly was," Mary said.

Nat Elias was searching his pockets. "Sam, you got a cigar in the house?"

Sam said, "No, I'm sorry – I forgot – I should have – you got any next door?"

Nat said, "No, I ran out." He started to lift himself to his feet. "I'll go down – "

Dave was there. "I'll go. Gotta get some fresh air."

"Okay! Good idea! Get me the panatelas!"

"I know, I know!"

After his brother had gone, Nat said, "With him you never know."

Sam said, "He's okay."

"Sure, sure, but yesterday I asked him what subjects he's taking. You should have heard the answer! Philosophies, with religion, with mishmash! I guarantee, with all of it, in twenty years you couldn't net twenty dollars."

Harriet said, "He's doing what he always wanted to do. That's important."

"Okay, okay, who's stopping him? Hey, where's the floor show?"

In the confusion Mark and his sister had left the room; Sam went to the hallway. "Mark?"

"Pretty soon, Papa," came the distant answer.

"I've never seen such a buildup to music," Nat Elias muttered, repositioning himself comfortably. "That reminds me, where's the thing what won the prize? I never did get to see it."

"Don't ask me. You'll have to ask the boy scientist," Sam told him.

Mary Elias said, "He made a – an oscilloscope for – for wave-form analysis."

Sam grinned, "Listen to her! So now you know!"

Nat said defensively, "Sure I know! They had one in *Popular Mechanics* in the ads. War surplus."

"Oh, he didn't buy it," Mary said quickly. "He built it!"

Sam's face was split wide with a grin. "Yeah! For five thousand bucks! Out of a five-dollar electronics set we got him for his birthday last year!"

Harriet turned to Sam. She said somberly, "Remember that time I saved up and bought you that chemistry set you wanted? I've wondered and wondered. What did Mama do with it when she took it away from you?"

Sam's face was suddenly weary. "I don't know. . . ."

"Why? Why?" Her words were thin blades. "I keep asking myself again and again. Why did she have to be like that – why? – driving Pa to suicide – "

Sam said sharply. "Shut up! The kids!"

Harriet said softly, "When I was a kid, I wanted to love her so much. . . ."

Mary Elias sat looking at them, at the old pain in their faces.

Nat said, "I keep asking myself again and again – is she really – is all that – " He made a gesture of finality.

"I wish I knew . . ." said Harriet.

Sam's eyes lost their inwardness. He said sharply, "What do you mean by that?"

Harriet's words were a whisper: "The way she died . . ."

"What are you talking about?" Sam demanded.

Nat said harshly to his sister, "Heart attack! You know that as well as I do!"

"I don't know . . ." said Harriet.

"What's on your mind?" Nat demanded. "Go on!"

"Yeah! Say it!" Sam demanded.

"She was always so healthy," Harriet said.

"Will you listen to her!" Nat exclaimed. "With a heart attack who knows? Healthy one minute and the next – " He snapped his fingers.

"I was with her all the time," Harriet told them.

Nat exclaimed, "So you were with her all the time!"

"What is it, Sis?" Sam asked her. "Why do you – "

"I keep thinking about it. . . . It was as if suddenly she wanted to be somewhere else. . . ."

They sat in silence, the family Elias. Finally Sam said, "I gotta admit somethin'. I haven't wanted to say it before. But that's the way it seemed to me, too. . . ."

"What in hell's the matter with you two?" Nat demanded. "I talked to the doctor! A heart attack is a heart attack!" He turned to his brother. "I'm going to tell you something about this sister of yours! She thinks I don't know, but I'll tell you! She's been going screwball, visiting those fakers, those mediums, or whatever they're called!"

Harriet said, "You don't know what you're talking about!"

"Don't try to bluff it out!" Nat said. He turned to Sam and Mary. "About a month ago I'm sittin' in the office – thank God nobody's around – so when the telephone rings I answer it myself. It's some old woman with a deep voice. The name she gives is Madam Astrid, somethin' like that – "

At the name Harriet had stiffened; Nat saw the reaction and he said, "That's the one, eh?" He turned back to the others. "So she wants to know if Harriet's there. I tell her no. So she wants to know who I am, so I think it's a friend, a customer, so I tell her. Then begins the big sales pitch! She's havin' a big whatchama-callit? – special séance – that night, and she wants me to let Harriet know and I should come with Harriet because she's positive that this is the night she's gonna communicate, like she says it, with 'Our dear departed.' Can ya beat it? At her age throwin' away good money to sit around in the dark holdin' hands with screwballs and phonies!"

Sam Elias turned to his sister. "Harriet, is this true?"

She nodded her head wordlessly.

"Why?"

"Yeah!" Nat demanded. "Didn't you, of all of us, have enough of her in *life*?"

Mary's hands were outstretched. "Please – the children – "

Sam Elias took a deep breath. He said with deliberate quietness, "They *are* phonies, you know. They really are. Remember when I was going to school I worked for a coupla summers in Ocean Park?"

Nat nodded. "Yeah, sure!"

"Well, I met this spiritualist, fortune-telling dame there" – a quick glance at Mary – "she – uh – kinda liked me, and one night she gave me the whole inside angle. How they let you talk and they listen and they pick up angles on things you say without your knowing you said them, and then they give you the answers you want based on what you told them."

Nat said harshly, "It's a disgrace that we even should have to talk about it! A grown woman!"

"What's the disgrace?" Sam demanded. "So she went, so lotsa people do! Harriet, do you know that there's companies that make a business of selling those spirit things? They send out regular catalogs full of recordings of spirit voices, and tables that give off ghost sounds, and gimmicks so they can move things at a distance, and wigs and masks and sheets that shine in the dark. Believe me, it's strictly a racket!"

Harriet said softly, "I only went the one time. . . ."

"But why?" Nat wanted to know. "*Why* did you go?"

Her eyes were unfocused. "I don't know. . . ."

Nat mocked, "'I don't know'! Listen, I'm going to say one thing more and that's all! When we moved out of that damn house and gave away every bit of that furniture, every bit of her clothes, and everything else, it ended for me, and for you! So no more of that Madam Astrid stuff! Do you hear me?"

She said docilely, "Yes, Nat."

"Okay!" He settled back into his chair once more. "Where's Dave and those damn cigars! Now if I could straighten *him* out!"

Mary said, "Be patient."

"Yeah, yeah!"

Sam said, "That was a mighty cute little girl that was up here."

Nat said, "Who was that?"

Sam laughed. "Come on now! You're still breathing!"

Nat said, "Oh, that reporter!"

Sam said, "To quote you – yeah, yeah!"

Mary said, "I thought she was a very striking girl. And she seemed very competent." She looked at Harriet. "Beautiful black hair, don't you agree?"

Harriet said quietly, "I liked her."

Nat said, "We'll wait until we see what she writes." The door sounded. He called out, "Well! So you made it!"

The walk had burned out some of the alcohol; Dave Elias's deep-set eyes were alert as he said, "I didn't do you much good. He was outta panatelas. I got you these."

Nat took the foil-wrapped cylinders; he said grudgingly, "Okay. They'll do fine."

He placed the containers on the end table alongside of his chair. He sighed deeply, his face a relief map of deepened crevices.

Dave stood there looking down at his brother; his head slowly turned to take in the other somber faces. He said, "Whassamatter? No, let me guess. Two to one somebody mentioned Mama!"

Nat said, "You're so funny!"

Dave strode to the center of the half circle. "Whassamatter with all of you? She's been dead for six months and eight days, so who invited her to the party?"

Sam said, "Sit down, Dave, please!"

"It's a party, so make it a party!" Dave went on, "I'm alive at last, and you're alive, and Harriet – " He grinned at her. "Did she tell you she's finally got a boy friend? A regular Mr. Don Juan. With a hairpiece!"

Harriet said savagely, "Shut up!"

"Well, facts are facts!"

"Shut up!"

Sam said, "Okay, let's all take it easy!"

Dave threw up his hands. He slumped into a nearby chair.

Again the oldest brother sighed deeply. He said, "Sam, I want to ask you something. All these months – I never asked you – but now that we're all here and on the subject, why not?" The others all looked at him intently. "Since I was the only one who wasn't there at her bedside – did she say anything – you know – at the very end? You know, any last words or anything? I'd like to know."

In the stillness Mary Elias suddenly heard the high singing note from down the hall. Experimenting now? Yes, better they weren't in here.

Nat Elias looked around at the tight faces. He rose to his feet. "Okay. So what did she say? I'm entitled to know!"

Harriet spoke. Her face was like a clenched fist. "A terrible thing!"

Her older brother turned to her. "So you did know! I asked you weeks ago! Why didn't you tell me?"

"A terrible thing!" Harriet repeated.

"Say it!"

Mary Elias said, "No – "

"Say it!"

Dave said, "Okay! Her last words were, 'I want you – '"

"Stop!" Mary Elias pleaded.

"Mary," Sam said.

"For Pete's sake, *say it!*" Nat demanded.

Dave said, "I'm telling you! She said, 'I want all of you with me soon. Tell Mark and Shirley.'"

"Dear God!"

Harriet said tearfully, "And she knew what she was saying!"

Nat Elias slowly moved back to his chair. He sat down carefully, infinitely old and weary. After a long, pulsing silence he turned to Mary Elias who sat, face stricken, hands clasping and unclasping in her lap.

He said, "Mary, I'm sorry. But how do you apologize for the devil? She was never a mother – not for one minute – why she had us – to torture us, I guess – Sam must have told you – "

"But to talk of her in such a way!" Mary Elias cried out. "She was still your mother!"

"Mother!" Harriet Elias spat the word. Then she put her face into her cupped hands and wept.

Dave Elias's face, now, was bright with excitement. He said, "At last we're talking about it! All right, I'll tell you something else. Don't look for reasons, excuses for Mama! Sure, I've read the books – when someone is like she was, you're supposed to go back to the genes, the chromosomes, in her mind, the glands, some kind of sickness! But not Mama! She wasn't sick that way! She knew exactly what she was doing until the minute she died!"

Mary Elias burst out, "There is good in everyone!"

"Stop being naïve!" Dave told her furiously. "Look around you at the world! Centuries of wars – mountains of dead – a new war waiting to burn us like a match, and still we go around saying, 'There's good in everyone!' Listen, you all know everything about me! You know that I'm a religious man! I believe that God makes good and he makes evil! All right! Some of us are a mixture of a little of each. But just as there are a few people on earth who are all good – saints on earth! – I tell you that there are devils on earth! Yes, Nat was right – Mama was a devil! I say it, and I know it, and I believe it!"

In the pulsing silence Mary Elias thought, I can't stand it anymore! Their faces! Their tortured faces!

Suddenly Shirley was in the room, followed this time by Mark, and he was carrying a large roll of recording tape.

"We've got it, Mama," Shirley said brightly.

Smiles carved into gray faces; Harriet hurriedly wiped her eyes and said, "How nice! We're going to have music!"

Dave said, "This I'm gonna like!"

Nat said, "It better be good! I'm tired out waiting."

Sam said, "You leave it to Mark. It'll be something special, believe me!"

As the small boy bent over the apparatus, Nat beckoned to Sam. He said *sotto voce*, "Isn't that the same tape recorder *she* gave them for Christmas?"

Sam said uncomfortably, "Yeah. So it's theirs. I let them do what they want with it."

Mark called out, "It's ready now, please."

Sam said, "Okay! Everybody get a good seat."

"Look at me!" Dave said. "I got the best seat in the house! I gotta friend knows the producer!"

"What kind of music did you record, Mark?" Harriet asked. She wiped at her cheek with the back of her hand.

Dave said, "Soul music! I only listen to soul music!"

Nat said impatiently, "Okay, turn it on. Turn it on!"

Sam said, "Go ahead, Mark. Everybody's waiting."

"Yes, Papa," said the boy. He flipped a switch; a burst of sparks and the overhead chandelier lights winked out.

"What the hell – " Nat rumbled.

"Turn on the lights!" Harriet's voice shrilled. *"Turn on the lights!"*

A chair crashed; an oath; Sam's voice: "Stand still! Stay where you are! I'll get lights!"

"I'll turn them on, Papa," Mark said loudly. "They're on different circuits."

A floor lamp went on: the sudden glare spotlighted Dave on the floor still entangled in a chair, with the others frozen as if in a child's game.

Sam moved. He said, "What's the matter with all of you! Just a fuse!"

"I'm sorry, Papa," Mark said. He hurried toward the door. "I'll go fix it."

Mary Elias put comforting arms around her sister-in-law. "It's all right, dear. No reason to be upset."

"I know," Harriet said through her tears. "I'm sorry."

Nat Elias took a deep breath. "So! For this they paid him five thousand dollars, the boy genius!"

Sam had been busily turning on sidetable lamps. He said, "Will you simmer down? Anybody can blow a fuse. Plenty of other lights."

Mary Elias turned to Dave. "You all right?"

"Sure, sure, but I kinda wrecked the chair."

"Don't worry about it."

"A kid that size monkeying with electricity!" Nat snorted.

The overhead lights beamed on; everyone looked up at the miracle as Mark came back into the room. He said, "I'm sorry, Papa. It was just that the wire came loose from the screwhead and shorted out the other lead. I'll have it fixed in a minute."

Nat Elias was on the move. "It's gettin' very late – "

Sam said, "You heard him. He'll get it fixed in a minute. Sit down, will ya?"

Grumbling, the oldest brother reseated himself. The others followed his example.

Dave said, "This better be good."

"I'm sure it will be," Mary Elias stated. "Harriet. You all right?"

"Yes . . . but – please – don't turn out the lights again."

"He won't, he won't," Sam reassured her. "Just a shorted wire. He's fixing it."

Mary Elias lifted Shirley into her lap. She bent down to the child. "Tell me confidentially – is it going to be pretty music?"

Shirley looked up at her smiling mother. She said seriously, "It's not exactly music, Mama. . . ."

Robin Shepherd wiped the cleansing cream off her face. The bath mirror blurred from the steam of her bath; she flicked a tissue out of the box and cleaned the condensation away. She thought, now why do I want to see that face more clearly? It hasn't changed. Wide-eyed, Simple Simon face. Why can't it be green-eyed, gaunt, hollow-cheeked, full of mysteries and inner wisdoms?

Look at it! The face of what I am! A little pink-and-white girl out of her time, out of her place. What was my time and place? It was with you, Howard! So safely with you!

The mirror misted again – this time it was because her eyes blurred. Dear God, when will I have no more tears?

She dabbed at her eyes and turned toward her bed. In the far distance an ambulance siren wailed of misery. Whoever it is, she thought, may they know no pain.

She got under the sheet and pulled the blanket high under her chin.

And if they die, may they have that final moment to say good-bye.

She closed her eyes and took a deep shuddering breath. Enough. She would think of her day. That foolish old man, Mr. Barnet, reaching for someone to ease his fright of the tumbling years. That Mr. Dumont, young Abe Lincoln with a cynical recorder. Harriet Elias whispering, "You are a sensitive." Sensitive to what? The heat? The darkening room? "Sensitive!" cried out an old voice, and suddenly she remembered. That shrouded fool on that dusty stage . . . No, wouldn't think of that! Think of Bob Farrell, of laughter and beauty, but almost at once he became Howard, and she wept and wept, and suddenly she was windblown on the shores of Lake Waconia at the place where they had walked the day before he had left. She remembered his dark, high-cheekboned face – "There's a family rumor that my great-great-grandmother was raped by a Kiowa" – the kisses and the deepening kisses – her tears – (such different tears!) – his confident "I have a gift for survival, darling. I'm sure the Marine Corps can use an All State halfback on its Service Team."

The air had been very still as she stood there in her agony. Then a whisper. Who had whispered? There was no one. The beach was empty. She called out his name; it echoed faintly, thin as a distant bird's call. She fell to her knees in her agony. It was not ended! It couldn't be ended! That face, that strength, all that he was and that she had loved – surely God could not let it end so quickly! Surely the dead, the young dead, the sacrificial dead, were entitled to a farewell, a last kiss, a look, a final touch!

She opened her eyes and through the blur of tears she saw where she was, in a small room that was now her home, and she said a quick prayer, and the children were there. Always, before, they had been like the sun-edged mist, but now they were firm, real, the faces of Shirley and Mark Elias, those dear, dear, children. They smiled at her and as the half sleep became blessed sleep, Harriet Elias was bending over her, whispering, whispering into the crawling darkness edged with red.

Nat Elias blew his nose and said, "One more minute, then I *am* going. Do you realize how late it is? After eleven!"

Sam said, "He's ready, he's ready!"

Dave called out, "Start the floor show, boy! I paid a cover charge!"

"Turn it on, son," Sam said.

The boy had stationed himself directly in front of the apparatus. He said, "Well, first, it's kind of an invention."

"Invention!" repeated his father proudly and looked triumphantly over at his oldest brother.

"Not yet thirteen years old!" scoffed Nat Elias.

"So how old was that Canadian kid when he invented aluminum?" Sam demanded.

"And Mozart," said Mary Elias. "How old was he?"

"But look," Nat persisted, "it's nothing but a tape recorder, with a box with extension wires. Look – look!"

Sam had to shout to be heard over the torrent of cross conversation. "Please, everybody! Will you let the boy play the machine?" In the grumbling silence he turned to his son, "Okay, Mark. Go ahead."

Mark said, "Do you mind if I say something before I turn it on?"

"Such a polite boy," said Aunt Harriet.

Sam said, "Of course, Mark, say what you want."

The door chimes closed the boy's mouth; Nat groaned as Mary Elias said, "Who now?"

Sam said, "Let's ignore it!"

But when the chimes persisted, he left the room, to return, a few moments later, telegram in hand. "Who in the heck is Cousin Morris?" he wanted to know.

Mary Elias said, "Cousin Morris?" and the name echoed from the others.

"Yeah, listen to this!" Sam said. "'My heartiest congratulations on the great honor which has come to you and the family today. May your son's future be as bright as his present.' And it's signed, 'Cousin Morris and family.'"

"Is there an address?" Nat asked. "Is there a city?"

Sam examined the telegram. "Baltimore, Maryland. That's all."

Mary said, "There's nobody on my side of the family in Baltimore, Maryland."

Sam turned to his sister. "Who've we got in Baltimore, Maryland?"

Harriet shook her head negatively.

Dave said, "Wait a minute! Isn't he the one on Pa's side who had the clothing store – "

"No. That was in Philadelphia." Nat told her.

Dave said, "Wasn't there a tall, thin woman with a mole who used to come over to the house when we were little who married – "

Sam said, "That's the one who got killed in that automobile accident. She never got married."

Mary Elias said, "It *must* be someone on my side of the

family! I had an uncle who got married again after his first wife died and – no, he never lived in Baltimore. They all went West to San Francisco years ago."

Sam fingered the yellow paper. He said, "Well, Cousin Morris and family, whoever you are – "

In the beat of silence that followed, Harriet spoke. She said, "Maybe it was somebody on Mama's side. . . ."

For another breath no one reacted. Then Nat snorted, "What're you talking about? Just to hear yourself talking? What relatives did we know of Mama's? Name me one! Just one! As far as we're concerned, Mama *had* no relatives! And you know it!"

"But – but everybody has relatives," Mary Elias exclaimed.

Dave said grimly, "Not Mama!"

Mary Elias said, "But that's nonsense! Surely she – "

Sam broke in loudly; he said, "Sure, sure, but she never talked about them, so we know nothing about them."

"Then this could be one," Mary Elias persisted.

Sam spoke quietly, firmly. "Mary."

Mary Elias got the message. "I'm sorry. . . ."

Sam turned to his son still standing before the apparatus. "I guess we're ready now. You were starting to tell us something?"

Uncle Nat said gruffly, "Yeah, go ahead, Thomas Edison."

Mark said, "I thought maybe you'd like me to explain how it works."

"We know already." Dave grinned. "You plug it in and it blows out a fuse."

"Dave!"

Dave Elias put up a palm of peace at his brother. "All right, all right!"

"Go ahead, Mark," Sam said with finality. "There'll be no more interruptions."

"Thank you, Papa." He turned to the others. "It's true that this part is an ordinary tape recorder, but I have made certain modifications." He touched the smaller container. "What is important is this. You know, of course, about the law of the conservation of energy."

Dave Elias did a comic "take" at the others, and Sam grinned at his older brother. He said, "Well, Nat?"

"So what am I – a Yale professor?" growled Nat Elias.

The boy went on: "The law says that the total energy of any body is a quantity which can be neither increased or diminished, though it may be transformed into any one of the forms of which energy is susceptible."

"I'll vote for that, kid!" Dave announced.

Sam's proud look was echoed in Mary Elias's face.

"So it seemed kind of logical to me," Mark went on, "that if nothing in nature is lost, it should be possible to bring back voices, since voices are sound waves, and sound waves are energy."

Nat consulted his watch. He said, "It's very late. I've got a big day tomorrow."

Sam said, "Now look, Nat, he's your only nephew. At least be courteous!"

"All right, all right!" To the boy: "So voices are energy, so what?"

"I can bring back voices," Mark told him.

"What voices?"

"Yes, Mark, what voices?" Sam asked.

"Old voices," Mark told him.

Nat Elias shook his head wearily.

"Yeah, boy, you'd better explain that one!" Dave exclaimed.

"But I did," Mark said. "The law of nature that says nothing is lost. Just changed, but it's all there. You burn a match and it divides into various gaseous compounds, but those gases aren't lost. And so the match isn't lost."

"All right, all right," Nat grated, "but we're not talking about matches. You said voices!"

"In theory it's the same thing," the boy told him. "Everything is basically electrical. Whether it's a gas or the vibrations of the human voice, if you break it down, it's all a matter of electro-magnetic waves. So I got to thinking about it and I think I've figured out a way to bring back old voices."

Nat said disgustedly, "Old voices! There he goes again!"

"What old voices?" Sam asked his son.

Mark looked at all of them. Then he said simply, "The voices of the dead."

In the sudden silence Nat Elias labored to his feet. He said,

"So I'm discourteous! Am I supposed to stay around to listen to that science-fiction crap – excuse me – all right, I got excited! – do I have to listen to that science junk he stole off a TV program?"

"Yeah, where did you get that screwy idea, boy?" Dave Elias wanted to know. He, too, was on his feet.

"Yeah, I'd like to know that myself!" Sam Elias said. "Where did you get such an idea?"

"From Grandma," Mark Elias told them.

The room became a silent tomb.

"Grandma?" Harriet's question was a whisper in the emptiness.

Nat Elias lumbered forward toward the boy. He said, "What the devil you talking about? Answer me! Come on! Answer me!"

Dave joined him in demands; Mary Elias told them not to talk so loudly; Sam shouted over all of them until their hubbub subsided. Then he said, "All right, so he said something crazy!" He turned to his son. "Mark, what do you mean, Grandma told you? When did she tell you such a thing?"

Mark looked over at his sister still seated in her mother's lap. Then he said, "A long time ago."

"When?" his father demanded.

"When we were over at her house once, Shirley and me."

Shirley grinned and nodded her head in agreement.

"He's crazy!" Nat exclaimed. "What did Mama know about science and stuff like that?" He turned to the boy. "What are you lying for? What are you after?"

Mark said mildly, "Can I turn it on now, Papa?"

Nat Elias swung his anger toward Sam. "He's your kid! Make him answer!"

Sam looked in confusion toward Mary, then he tried to smile. He said, "I – I think the best answer is he should turn it on. It's a joke, that's all, isn't it, Mark?"

A small firm hand clicked a switch and plastic reels whirlpooled.

The Elias family was an ear focused on the loudspeaker. Only Shirley sat disinterested, her eyes beyond the windows on a tiny airplane slanting in for a landing at a distant airport.

A faint rushing sound began, like wind through pine needles, then a thin whistle, rising and falling over and over again in wave-form rhythms. "Hey," exclaimed David Elias, "he's tuned in on my old superhet radio set!"

Tension broke into laughter. Quick words splattered to cover uneasiness.

Sam said loudly to his oldest brother, "I told you! A kid's joke! So what did you get so excited about?"

Shirley's head swiveled from plane viewing to the loudspeaker as over the whistle began a sound like the beat of an angry finger on a drumhead.

"Now he's got the sound of old popcorn!" Dave chortled.

Nat Elias got to his feet. He smiled patronizingly. He said, "Well, this has been very nice, but I really got to get to bed. I've got those wholesalers from Kansas City coming in at nine in the morning and I – "

A cat cried out. Distantly, as if in a memory.

They were wax figures in a tableau. Their eyes were frozen rods caught in the loudspeaker's grille.

Again the cat called out, and again, closer and closer, a piteous creature seeking to be let in – begging, seeking, longing. . . .

"Turn it off!" Harriet's shriek lifted from her corded throat.

Nat Elias found voice. "What kind of a joke is this?" He turned toward the boy's father. "He's got a helluva sense of humor, your boy genius! He tape-records her goddam cat and now he plays it back to us! Very funny!"

Sam Elias looked dazedly at the now silent speaker, the revolving reels. He said, "Recording?"

Dave Elias ran a hand over the tremble of his mouth. He said, "Sure! Tape recording!"

A thin line of spittle drooled from Harriet's lips. "The cat was dead . . . before *she* gave them the recorder. . . ."

Only the children saw Uncle Nat's face go aflame; his eyes turned upward and, as he fell, he clawed at the tablecloth and everything went in on him, all the dishes with all their remnants of the sandwiches, the chocolate cake, and the wet pickles.

PART TWO

Chapter 5

In the morning, after she had her usual breakfast of three vitamins and a cup of coffee, Robin decided that she would do the Mark Elias story at once. There was no rush for it – the magazine had just gone to press – but it would be better to do the article now while the picture of the small boy was bright in her mind. And before she had to make a decision about the groping Mr. Barnet.

She suddenly remembered her illness in the Elias apartment, then she put the thought from her. It was morning and she felt – how had Bob Farrell put it? – like fresh roses at dawn.

She began her pre-writing ritual of pulling the small table over to the window so she could look out at the oleander bush; then she had to attach an extension cord in order to use her electric portable. By the time she did the furniture moving, the power plugging, the carbon paper insertions, filled a small dish with chocolate kisses, and placed her chair at exactly the right angle, generally she had thought out her lead so that she could begin the mechanics of hitting the keys at once.

But this day the formula fell apart. Although she took an inordinately long length of time to get started, the story, when she finally sat down to write, simply was not there. *The Southwestern Weekly* used oblique-angled articles; the only ideas that came to her now were definitely cube-shaped.

She tried the device of typing titles: "Hollywood Vunderkid"; "Nobel Prizer 2000 A.D."; "It Happened at 12" – they did nothing for her elusive muse.

Yet she knew the story was there – that marvelous small boy – that angel-faced sister – how stupid not to have an answer! She typed another title: "The Mark Elias Story." She added "By Robin Shepherd." So far, brilliant. She looked out the window. A blue jay snipped a leaf from the bush, found it bitter, protested to the universe, and winged off.

Robin began to type again: "At twelve years of age, Mark Elias looks for new worlds to conquer. Having just won the National Science Scholarship, this very small boy with a monumental IQ views the future with its vistas of Nobel prizes and – "

She tore the paper out of the typewriter, balled it up, and threw it over her shoulder as the telephone rang.

She picked up the receiver gratefully. "Hello?"

"Tony Dumont here!"

Oh, we do it in the British manner, do we? "Good morning, Mr. Dumont."

"Good morning. Have you started your small boy story yet?"

"I'm just at it," she told him.

"I dug up an interesting angle on the family. I'd like to come over and tell you about it."

Come over? She said, "I'm afraid that's impossible. I'm just leaving for an appointment. Could I meet you at your station later?"

Tony Dumont said, "Well, could I come over later?"

She said, "No, I don't think that's possible. I'll be in your neighborhood at two. You're with KQUB, aren't you?"

He said, "Yeah, okay, two it is."

She heard the click of the receiver falling in the cradle. Ha!

She turned back to the typewriter. She thought, someday they're going to find out about me. That article in the *Sunday Times* that got me the magazine job, an angel danced on my pen. But I'm not really a writer, I'm Mama's little girl sitting at a grown-up typewriter. If I pound the keys enough millenniums, something happens. If I were a real writer I would take the story of that wonderful boy and turn it into something with which every reader could relate, the miracle of a man and a woman's love coming together into the new entity of a beautiful child who has the potentials of greatness. Instead I sit here like a clump pecking out weary phrases.

The telephone rang again. Ah, what new scheme has *Canus wolfus* thought up now to get into my room?

"Hello?"

"Hello, there!" She recognized the voice at once – Bob Farrell. He wanted to know how she was; was she ready for another safari into a hot fudge sundae?

They talked pleasantly, easily, already good friends, and when he asked her if she would have dinner with him that evening, she was delighted and told him so.

After she had hung up, Robin saw that it had suddenly grown quite dark in the room; a fine rain was misting the windows. It was a good day in which to work, but when she turned back to her typewriter, all she could think about was which dress she should wear that night.

What nonsense! Anything would do! She decided that, come what may, she must start the article. Perhaps if she saw the children again, away from the distractions of the party atmosphere, her brain cells would function. Yes, and Harriet Elias – she could see her at the same time and solve the mystery of that whispered conversation.

She found the Elias phone number among her notes and dialed it. The telephone beep sounded, but there was no answer. She looked in the phone book for a Harriet Elias. It was not listed, but when she saw "Nat Elias" she remembered that was the name of the oldest brother. She carefully dialed the number, but again the distant bell rang unanswered.

She recalled that the family business was a toy company; she looked up "TOYS – WHOL. & MFRS.," in the classified directory. When her finger came to "Friendly Toy Company," she recalled the name. She dialed the listed number. When a girl answered, Robin asked if she might speak to either Mr. Sam or Mr. Nat Elias.

There was a moment's hesitation, then the switchboard operator said unclearly, "Mr. Sam Elias will not be in today."

"Nat Elias?" Robin persisted.

Again a split second's hesitation and the woman said, "Mr. Nat Elias died last night."

Robin thought, did I hear that? She managed to say, *"Nat Elias? Died? Are you sure?"*

The woman said wearily, "Yes. I am sure."

"What – what – "

"Are you a friend of the family?"

Robin said ambiguously, "I was with them last night. What happened?"

The woman said, "No one here seems to know whether it was a heart attack or a brain hemorrhage. It's all been so sudden." She was close to tears. "We're all very upset."

Robin told her that she would call back in a day or two. Telephone back in its cradle, she sat looking at it. That vigorous man – dead! The rain had freshened; it was beating mournfully on the window. Yet he had been gray, full of years. But Howard – she began to cry, and, furious at herself, she turned to the typewriter and began to write in a fury of deliberate concentration.

Shirley Elias was quite content. She sat on the thick cushion of the windowbox tracing the hide-and-go-seek of the raindrops down the glass. Behind her she could hear the rise and fall of the heterodyne note as the beloved one worked on the apparatus.

She said without turning, "Mark." At his answering grunt she went on, "Where did Papa go?"

"To make the arrangements," Mark told her.

"What are arrangements?" she wanted to know.

"The burning."

Her head swiveled sharply. "Burning?"

Mark turned the dial and the note deepened. "They call it cremation."

"Golly!" the small girl exclaimed. "When do they do it?"

"Tomorrow. In the morning." He turned the dial another fraction and the note was a soft growl.

Shirley jumped off the seat and came toward him. "Can we go? Can we watch?" she demanded excitedly.

"You bet!" her brother told her firmly. He turned the dial again and the note became subsonic, just beyond the range of hearing. Both children came closer and listened intently, heads cocked to the loudspeaker.

At one o'clock Robin sat in the windowseat looking at the angry downpour. She had typed for hours; now, fingers weary, she watched the rivulets of water crisscrossing down the glass.

The greenery beyond was clean-washed, eagerly lifting to the long-overdue rain.

The telephone; it was Tony Dumont: "It's two-thirty. I thought you were meeting me."

She had completely forgotten; he cut into her apologies with, "Look, I've found out something that's really important. To your story. I'll pick you up in front of your place twenty minutes from now. Okay?"

She could find no reason to refuse; she said, "Okay." Important? What could he know that was important to her? Yet a ride in the rain would be pleasant. Without thought or memory. She went to her closet to get her raincoat and her boots.

The freeway was a black river, but the cars, including the one she was in, were still hurtling along at the dry weather maximum. Robin realized that she had been wrong about no memory; after they had flashed by a few wrecks draped over the center divide, the flaming, crumpled smashup that had taken her parents was burning again behind her closed lids.

She felt the car turn; she opened her eyes to see, gratefully, that they were leaving the restricted highway; a street sign indicated "To Mulholland Highway."

She recalled that was the fabled lovers' lane of the Los Angeles area; she darted a quick glance at Tony Dumont. He was concentrating on the rain-swept, climbing road. Was that what was so "important"? A lovers' lane tussle in the rain?

As she began planning strategy, just in case, unexpectedly he said, "We are headed for Mulholland Highway. Not the 'Let's park the car and have fun' section of it, I assure you."

Robin relaxed inwardly, then said the expected, "It never entered my mind."

The road began to snake through cuts in the mountain ridge; the rugged slopes were covered with a tangle of bushes and small trees new green under the freshening rain.

He said, "This is forest fire country. The section I am taking you through has never been burned over."

Remembering the towering forests of home, she said, "It doesn't seem as if those bushes could sustain much of a fire."

He told her that most of that brush was greasewood; the nature of the bark was such that it burned with the ease and explosiveness of oily rags. Then he smiled. "We're safe in this rain."

Robin thought, well, that's reassuring. For a moment there I thought you were taking me out for a pyromaniac party. She suddenly exclaimed, "Look out!"

His face jerked to the road ahead; he cut the wheels sharply and a tiny cotton-tailed rabbit leaped to safety. Emptiness rushed at them; Tony pulled the steering wheel hard and the car balanced on the edge of a falloff, then settled back on the road.

When he looked at her, he said grimly, "Was Peter Rabbit *that* important to you?"

She did not speak; she nodded her head that it was important.

He looked at her unblinkingly; she felt her skin grow warm as his eyes searched her face. Finally he said, "When I first saw you I didn't quite believe. You have the sort of dewy white-and-pink face that one expects to be circled by wreaths of flowers held in the air by laughing cherubs. Yet here you are. In a two-bit arena full of knifers and grabbers and round-heels! Why?"

She quietly told him, "I don't think I know what you're talking about."

He lifted heavy eyebrows. He said, "Until further evidence is presented, I shall continue to dodge all rabbits. Anyway, it's about five minutes to doomsday for all of them." At her look, he went on, "The big dozers are coming. Unquote Warren Dorn."

"Who's he?" she asked.

"A friend of mine. He watchdogs these mountains. But, like your rabbits, he's already fighting a rearguard action."

She thought, it's very nice that he is concerned about conservation, but I don't understand – what has the decline and fall of the Southern California wilderness to do with the Elias story?

Tony Dumont swung the car to the side of the road; beyond the flat, the mountain fell starkly away to the sea. He set the emergency brake and turned the ignition key.

Robin rolled down the window at her side. The raindrops were tiny muted drums.

Tony Dumont said, "Can I assume you're from a small town?"
She nodded.

He said, "I am, too. We'll reminisce some other time. I've got a strong feeling that right now you're thinking some variation of what-the-hell-is-this-all-about."

Rain began to drift through the opening; Robin turned up the window and waited.

When Tony spoke again, his eyes were on a far point on the horizon. He said, "The water. It's an obsession of mine." She looked at him. "It's the same, you know. All that ever was at Creation is still with us. It rises from the land, and falls, and rises again. A liquid chain from then to now. From them to us." His hand went out to the glass of the wet windshield. "These very drops may have fallen on a thunder dinosaur." His voice tightened. "Or vaporized in the fire over Hiroshima." He looked down at her. "Or lifted off the kiss of lovers a thousand miles and a thousand years away." He suddenly put a forefinger to her face and ran it quickly down the curve of her cheek. He said softly, "I had to find out if that, at least, was for real." As Robin sat very still, very silent, he went on: "Before I tell you what it's all about, will you come meet a very special friend of mine? He's only minutes from here."

She thought, he's got such a very craggy face. And he is trying to be friendly. She said, "All right."

As they drove along, he said, "I'd better brief you on Budge Hart. I don't want to spring him on you without preparation. He looks like a great gray grizzly bear and was a good enough artist, in his time, to have had dozens of one-man shows in the best galleries, and he's been purchased by museums from the Guggenheim to the Tate. For the past two years he's been totally blind. There's the kindness of the Fates for you! A great talent like that blinded in a world full of twenty-twenty pimps!"

As the car continued up the winding canyon, Tony said, "It's a very unusual house. Built around a huge eucalyptus – I don't know how many years ago. It was Budge's studio when he could paint. Now he spends most of his time repelling the hippies who want to move in. By the way, when we get there, once you take a seat, try not to move around. He likes to talk directly to people, and once he's located them by their voices, if they move around it confuses him."

The house, when they came to it, was set back from the road in a grove of shaggy-barked eucalypti. As Robin got out of the car, she saw a very handsome colored woman getting into a sports car parked in the driveway. A yellow car door slammed angrily; a motor spun, caught, roared; rocks splattered in a wheel-spinning getaway.

"This is the path," Tony said. He led her along the gravel. "Before he found his talent, Budge, among other things, was an All-American tackle, a lineman on one of the early pro-football teams, a union organizer, and a really great art teacher."

When they came up to the weathered redwood house, Robin saw that one of the largest of the trees was, indeed, growing right through the roof of the place. As Tony reached for the huge bronze doorknocker, he said, "Now you can understand why every drop-out within a hundred miles has been trying to get into this place. It must have something to do with a tribal yen to live close to the Tree Spirits. Or free leaves for stuffing your pad."

At the pound of the knocker, a group of unseen crows high in a nearby tree protested vigorously at having their siesta disturbed.

A small panel slid back; a sepulchral voice said, "Get the hell away from that door or I'll blow your goddam head off!"

"Budge! It's Tony!"

Latches squeaked and the door went open. "Tony! Talk about ESP, I was just thinking about you! Hey, you got somebody with you?"

Tony grinned at Robin. He said, "He's got a built-in radar. It's a girl, Budge. She – "

"Say no more!" The door came open wider, and Robin saw a massive man in a sweat shirt and worn gray slacks. Faded lettering stated that the pullover was the property of the U.C.L.A. Athletic Department; the garment's tightness accentuated the great bulk of the man's shoulders. He was wearing dark glasses which contrasted with the tousled gray thatch of hair above a handsomely eroded face.

"Come in, come in, sit down, my pretty," the old man said. "If you're with Tony, I'm certain you must be pretty."

"She is," Tony told him. He led Robin inside.

She saw a miscellany of pillowed, comfortable chairs, all of them centered around the great trunk of the tree that bored through the center of the parasol roof.

"Sit down," the blind man ordered. "Anywhere."

Robin found a chair; she watched as the huge man skillfully threaded his sightless way through the furniture obstacles and seated himself in what, apparently, was his favorite chair. All the while, he and Tony talked in the rapid, verbal shorthand of old friends.

Tony suddenly exclaimed, "Gynephobia!"

The blind man snorted. "Can't you do better than that? 'The aversion to associate with women on any social level.' That's not your problem! Say, I'm sorry you missed my friend Annie."

Tony told him they had seen the girl getting into her car as they arrived.

The blind man grinned. "I hope she didn't crack the door glass. She was slightly steamed, to say the least. She's on a black-is-beautiful syndrome. I asked her how about a black snowfall? Or a black moonscape? Would she eat cotton candy made with black sugar? How about a glass of black *vin rosé?* What really vexed the lass was when I asked her to write me a love note on black paper wrapped around a dozen long-stemmed black roses." The amusement left his sightless face. He said softly, "I do not deny the beauty of black. But all colors are beautiful." He suddenly added, "Thanatomania!"

Robin puzzled as Tony screwed up his forehead, then said triumphantly, "'Neurotic obsession for reading obituaries.'"

"You've been studying, my boy!" Budge Hart exclaimed. "Better explain to your friend."

Tony turned to Robin. "It's a game we play. Definitions of aberrations. It began with a broadcast I did a few months ago. Ever since then we've been tossing them back and forth."

"I'm sure you haven't an aberration in your pretty head," the old man boomed at Robin. "Tell me about yourself."

"She's from a small town, been in Southern California less

than a year, writes pretty fair articles for *The Southwestern Weekly*," Tony told him.

"She hire you as her mouthpiece?" the blind man demanded.

"She's shy and innocent," Tony explained with a grin at Robin. "And for your information, she looks like a – well, like a pink-and-white rose."

Robin felt the familiar rush of warmth to her face as the blind man said, "I'm impressed." He spoke toward Robin. "Generally, in his descriptions, Tony's about as lyrical as a television commercial on acid indigestion." He turned to Tony. "That woman was here again today."

Tony said, "Which one?"

"*That* woman. The dog."

"Eventually you'll have to give in."

"The hell I will!" the blind man exclaimed. He turned to Robin. "What, in all that's rational, would I do with a Seeing Eye dog? Where would he lead me? Upstairs and downstairs and to the kitchen table?" He ran his hand over the gray hedge of his beard. "There's something about blindness that brings out an excess of good in people. I've been deluged with it. 'There but for the grace of God, etc.' Offers of dogs of all shapes and descriptions. Offers of free sound libraries with everything from Shakespeare to killer whales in ecstasy. Offers of trips to here, there, anywhere. Why does everyone want to drive me places? I like it here. Or if they insist on taking me on a journey, why must it always be the zoo or the Griffith Park Observatory? Why don't they offer me invitations to the Isle of Capri, or Costa de los Pinos, St. Moritz, or the Greek Isles? And one more thing – why must the fingers on the doorbell always belong to aged ladies? Why can't I get a do-gooder who is a lush, avid nineteen just bursting to bring happiness to a dirty old man?" He turned to a grinning Tony. "That reminds me. Someone read me an item that you may bring your drivel to TV."

Tony had found the second most comfortable easy chair; he stretched out his long legs as he answered, "I've got a responsibility to the private enterprise system, haven't I?"

"Don't you realize that if you step into that cathode quicksand, you lose all hope?"

Tony Dumont said, "When did I ever have any? It's the residuals I'm focused on."

The blind man said, "How many times do I have to tell you that in radio you've found your *métier*? I hate to admit it, but every once in a while, in those programs of yours, you actually make your reportage a kind of unique art form. The oblique look at the world conjured up in the listener's own mind. An essay in imagination. Splash the same material on the big glass tube and you'll be a disaster."

Tony looked over at Robin. He said, "Remember you talked about trial without jury? Or judge? Here's the principal exponent of the technique."

The blind man groaned. "Where have I been, in the Gobi Desert? I had years of television watching! From the old Baird sets down to the General's best color a couple of years ago! Hell, I bought the very first television outfit ever seen in L.A.! The tube was so small I used to hold a magnifying glass over it to see if it was a face or a fly speck!"

Tony said, "And Hopalong Cassidy galloped over the horizon to save Warner Baxter. Don't you know that television has progressed beyond that? They now expose navels!"

"I'm talking about *your* kind of programming! I heard one you did a few weeks ago. Purely by accident, I assure you. Thirty minutes of the city at night. A police desk sergeant at the hour of his retirement, an old janitor sweeping the sidewalk in front of City Hall, bored teen-agers at a hamburger stand, a midnight Mass, a young girl arriving in town at the Greyhound station – you wrote it, need I go on? I hate to say it to your ugly face, but it was a tone poem, pure and simple! What would that have been on television? Nothing! Pieces of film out of an old documentary! I didn't have to see that old janitor. He was in my mind, he was the old man I knew back in my home town who swept out our church. I didn't want to see that girl at the station. In my mind she was and always will be dewy-eyed and lovely."

Tony said, "I'll do visual things! A fakir doing the old Indian rope trick! Fire-walking! Burial alive!"

"Sure, sure, that's three programs, what'll you do for an encore? Visit the skeletons floating in the Titanic? Dive for pennies into Mount Vesuvius? Is that going to be the apogee of your career, piling sensation on sensation for the bar watchers?"

As the discussion swooped back and forth, Robin found herself relaxing more and more, the uneasiness in her growing smaller and smaller. She thought, yes, I like this. Friendly arguments – discussions about little things. My head is weary of the great issues – death and life and eternity and evil and demons – yes, forgive me, even of God. Let me just sit here, unseen, uninvolved. . . .

She heard Tony suddenly exclaim, "Skopophobia!" and the blind man's derisive, "You're slipping! We had that last week. 'Fear of spies and foreign agents.'" He turned to Robin. "Did you hear that classic program of Tony's when he did that tour of L.A.'s aberrations?" When she told him she had not, he went on: "I knew there were mixed nuts around, but after listening to that show, I bought another lock for the door. Do you know there are people in this town walking the streets, going to the supermarket, driving their cars, and all that, who live in the constant fear of a vacuum?"

"'Horror vacui,'" Tony offered.

"They live in mortal terror of being left alone in an empty house or an empty room. Some of them keep buying and buying to fill their rooms and their closets against the emptiness. Others keep on eating, afraid that if they stop, air will rush in and they'll explode!"

Robin looked toward Tony. He said, "He's talking fact! They refuse to have an operation for fear the doctor will take out all of their vital organs. If it's a man, he can't even make love for fear that loving will drain him and he'll pop like a balloon! Remember I told you this town attracts all the kooks of the spirit world? In the same way it seems to draw in everybody with phobias."

The blind man said, "Naturally! In cold climates they'd be too busy with anginal pains from shoveling the snowdrifts! Did I tell you about the woman I met with Acathisia?" He turned toward Robin. "She's a young person with this neurosis about sitting down. No chairs in the house. Hasn't sat down in years. She's firmly convinced that if she sits down all sorts of things will happen to her. So there's no in-between with her. She's either standing up or lying flat in bed."

Tony grinned. "I think I've met the lady."

"Now, mind you, these aren't hospital cases," the older man went on. "These are, you'll excuse the expression, supposedly normal people you might meet anywhere, any time. Take the aberration of ablutomania. You must have met some of those yourself. Constantly washing their hands. Hundreds of times a day."

Tony said to Robin, "Ammusia."

The old man said, "Oh, that's a beauty!"

Tony went on: "That's a person who can't repeat a melody two seconds after he hears it. Can't even recognize 'The Star Spangled Banner.' Can you imagine a musician afflicted with that? Well, I've met him and I had him on my program. I also did a piece on a businessman who, when it thunders, hides under his desk. He's got a master's degree, a top job, and a happy family, and he's perfectly rational about everything else, but thunder to him is the devil himself."

Robin felt very weary. She said in a small voice. "Forgive me, but I'm afraid I must be getting back."

Quick good-byes – the blind man wanted her to come again – and in a few moments they were out of the circular room and driving beyond the small grove of trees.

Tony Dumont asked, "Like him?"

Robin said, "Yes. I do. Very much."

"Good! Now I think it's about time I told you what it's all about."

Robin thought, oh, yes, indeed!

"I've read some of your stuff," he went on. "You can really write. That 'Old Dog' article a couple of weeks ago – Human interest without bathos. It's sort of fantastic about you. The way you look, you should be writing Mother's Day cards for Hallmark! Me, the way I look, I should be – well, I can't write – not in your league – but I can plot, outline, and research. Will you collaborate with me?"

Robin said quickly, "Collaborate? On what?"

"A book, on the Elias family."

She thought, I don't think I'm hearing him correctly. It must be the altitude.

He went on: "The more I've researched that family – and I've been doing it all day – newspapers – magazines – friends on the police department – the more intrigued I've become with the idea."

She thought, police department? What have the Eliases to do with the police?

"What I want to do is one of those semidocumentary books in the manner of *In Cold Blood*. The inside-out story of a strange family. How does that strike you?"

She said, "I don't know what you're talking about. Forgive me, but do you?"

He said, "Collaborate. It means – "

"I know what it means! But I don't know what you mean when you talk about the 'strange' Elias family. They're a conventional middle-class American family who happen to have a very bright little child in their midst."

He looked at her in a sort of wonder. "Is *that* all you know about them?"

She said, "What should I know?"

"Didn't you do your homework?" At her continued blank look: "Didn't you look them up at all before you started your article?"

She shook her head.

He said, "My God, I thought you were a professional writer!"

She flushed; she said defensively, "A small boy wins a prize and I'm assigned to do a story on him. I interview him and his family. I consider that quite sufficient."

"Oh, do you?" he mocked. "Don't you consider it germane to your story that seven years ago that boy's grandmother went on trial for a sensational murder? Or that two years ago the grandfather of that boy committed suicide in one of the most fantastic manners in the history of suicide? What kind of writer are you, anyway?"

Robin felt an unaccustomed rush of words. "You're the judge and jury, so you tell me! And that reminds me – was the grandmother convicted of murder?"

Tony Dumont blinked. He said, "Well, no. Not exactly."

She pressed her advantage. "What sort of conviction is a 'no, not exactly'? Was she or wasn't she convicted of the alleged crime?"

He said, "She got off on a technicality! But she was guilty as hell!" At her look: "If you'd read a few newspapers of that time, the way I did this morning, you'd know what I'm talking about."

She said, "Oh, I understand completely! You look around you and you see that a certain type of book has been making a great deal of money for the author. So you say to yourself, 'That's for me!'"

"Now wait a minute –"

"So you meet this family and you say to yourself, 'Here's the money pot I've been looking for! Boy genius out of a murderer grandmother!' The fact that the woman was acquitted would spoil your story, so you conveniently ignore it! In other words, you want to write that book the way you do your broadcasts. If the material doesn't fit your preconceived story angle, the devil with facts, you can always doctor the tapes!"

He said, "That's a bitchy thing to say, Miss Shepherd!"

She said, "I don't like you, Mr. Dumont. Shall I walk back or will you drive me to a cabstand?"

He growled in his throat, turned the car with a spinning of tires, then shot the vehicle down the road.

Robin kept her eyes closed until they were back on the freeway. She expected that he would take her to her door, but instead, as soon as they were in the Valley, he stopped at the first cabstand, reached over, opened her door, and waited, as Robin, tight with anger, got out. She heard the door slam behind her and the insolent exhaust of the receding engine.

As she got into the waiting taxi, she thought, collaborate with you, Mr. Dumont? Only on your obituary! And then she was very ashamed of the thought; she took a deep breath and settled back in the seat. She suddenly thought, he talks about my not knowing facts! Why, he doesn't even know that Nat Elias is dead!

A half hour after she got home, the telephone rang.

"Hello?"

"This is Foot-in-his-mouth. I wanted you to know I'm sorry."

She said, "All right."

Tony Dumont said, "No, it really isn't. May I take you out to dinner?"

She said, "I'm afraid not."

"Oh, come on, now, surely forgiveness is one of your gentle virtues."

"I'm sorry. I have a date."

He said, "Oh, really! Make it a double-date, me and your anger."

She said precisely, "I am not angry, Mr. Dumont. I'm meeting with my photographer, Mr. Farrell. Now if you'll excuse me – "

He said gruffly, "Okay."

She heard the click of the broken connection. She thought I *am* angry! Why did I say I wasn't? I do not lie. She said a quick prayer asking for forgiveness.

Chapter 6

Darkness gloomed beyond the curved windows.

Sam said, "We'll talk as soon as Mary brings in the drinks, okay?"

David Elias did not answer. The overhead light gleamed on the wetness of his thin face as he looked out into the night.

"You got a fever or something?" Sam asked him.

Without turning his head, David shook it negatively.

"The way you're sweating," Sam said. "I've had the G.I.'s all day myself. Well, it's to be expected. Ah, Mary, come on, come on, we need the schnapps!"

Glasses settled on the coffee table. Mary thought, he's so tense. All day. Everything's a crisis. Maybe after the cremation. . . .

Sam drank deeply. He sighed. He said to his brother, "Drink up. Do you good."

David Elias said, without looking at them, "Where's Harriet?"

Sam and Mary exchanged a quick look. Sam said quickly, "She went out with Mr. Alt. For a ride. Mr. Alt insisted."

Mary said, "She's taking it very hard. She hasn't said a word all day."

Sam said, "I got a phone call from Mr. Margolis today."

Mary said, "Sam, must you?"

"For Pete's sake, do you think I want to talk about it?" Sam demanded. "But Mr. Margolis said the papers can't wait for signing. Something about the probate and taxes." He turned toward his brother. "Mr. Margolis told me that Nat had left everything to the kids." At Mary's gasp: "Yeah, to Mark and Shirley. In trust until they're of age, of course. With you and me," addressing his brother, "as trustees." He looked at Mary. "His share of the business. Of the house."

Mary said quickly, "I had no idea!"

Sam said, "Who did?"

Mary said, "I'm sorry, David."

He looked at her with a puzzled look as if he had not been listening: she saw that the skin below his eyes was darkened in semicircles of mourning.

He spoke to her, so softly that she had to strain to hear him.

"I was walking down a street," he said. "I went in. A church."

Sam said sharply, "What church?"

"I don't know." Weary eyes stared into the black beyond the windows. "I went in. I sat down. For a long time. All at once I knew. I really *knew!*"

"Knew what?" Sam demanded.

Mary said gently, "Tell us, David. Please."

The face he turned to her, she saw, was full of amazement.

"Don't you *know?*" he asked her. "*You?*"

She said soothingly. "Yes, yes, of course I do!" and she saw some of the tension leave him. He got to his feet.

Sam said, "You're not going?"

"He needs rest," Mary said. "Would you like to stay here tonight, David?"

The tortured mask shook negatively, moved with the thin, unsteady body toward the door.

Sam went after him. "David, about the – the legacy. Don't worry. We'll make it up to you out of our share. Okay, Mary?"

Mary said, "Of course."

"After all," Sam said, "what the hell do the kids need with a piece of the business? Uh – about tomorrow. We'll pick you up, okay? We're supposed to be there by eight-thirty."

David Elias was at the door. Sam added quickly. "Before you go, I want you to know I've decided you were right. What you talked about. Having Mark go to synagogue. Will you take him there this Saturday?"

David Elias turned his face toward Mary Elias, and he smiled fleetingly, and she knew he was saying to her that Sam did not know, only she and he knew.

But Mary Elias did not know, and when her brother-in-law had gone and Sam began a rush of small talk, she did not hear him as she listened, because she was just a little frightened, and she did not know why she was frightened.

As they drove away from her apartment house, Robin told Bob Farrell about Nat Elias's death.

"What a terrible shock to the family," he said. "Those poor children!" (She thought, what empathy!) "I know when my father died and I went home for the funeral, it appeared to me that all the adults were concerned about were the estate and the cost of the funeral. I was so emotionally shaken up by it all that I didn't function rationally for months."

Robin thought, yes, what a wonderfully sensitive person!

The word "sensitive" triggered off the memory of Aunt Harriet and her whispered comments in that overheated circular room the evening before; at Robin's silence, Bob said, "Forgive the cliché: A time for living and a time for dying. Let's say farewell to Mr. Elias and talk about living things. Such as where would you like to go. For dinner."

Robin thought split seconds, then she said, "Fairfax Avenue."

At his obvious amazement, she told him that the cooking there was the closest approximation to what it had been on the oilclothed kitchen table back home in Minnesota.

He said, "Great with me." He made a left turn. "We'll go Laurel Canyon." The car accelerated. "I thought the old folks at home were German."

She told him that her ancestry were German Lutheran, and Welsh Methodist, but just as Yiddish was a polyglot language, so was Jewish cooking the synthesis of the cuisine of the many countries in which the Jews had wandered; there was a chef on Fairfax who cooked as if he had been trained in her paternal grandmother's Stuttgart kitchen.

She noted the skill with which he maneuvered the car through the hill cuts green with the quick spring grass. He said, "Are you that interested in food?"

She told him that she enjoyed adventures in eating; beyond that, once in a while she had a nostalgic yearning for the childhood wonders of boiled chicken and thick soup and apple strudel.

"My question wasn't intended to be critical," Bob told her. They had crossed Sunset Boulevard and were in the bumper-to-bumper evening traffic of Fairfax Avenue. "I think it's great that you think, you'll pardon the expression, with your belly once in a while. I can't tolerate people who try to give you the impression that they eat only by osmosis."

Robin smiled, "You'll regret that remark when you get the check."

He chuckled, and Robin thought, I do like the way his blue eyes join his laughter.

She said, "By the way, how did the children's pictures turn out?"

He sighed. "I was hoping you wouldn't ask me that." At her startled look, he smiled ruefully. "I blew that one. It doesn't happen to me often, but when I do!"

She asked him what he meant; he told her, "The adults' pictures were fine, but I didn't get a single one of the kids. The shutter on my Rollei must have jammed. Every time I shot the children! Isn't that one for the book?"

She told him that it really didn't matter; she was a long way from the final draft of her story.

He said, "Great! I'll go back in a few days and pick up the kids' shots with my Leica. It's the damnedest thing! I develop all my own pictures, so I know the trouble wasn't in the processing. Happened to me only one time before. I had an assignment to cover a sexpot starlet at a pro football game – sitting on the players' bench and all that jazz. I got great shots – except for one thing. I forgot to take the dust cap off my lens!" He guided the car into the restaurant parking place. "I still can't figure it out about those kids. Why should that shutter work on every shot but theirs?"

Mary thought, we need a new mattress. The one thing we didn't change when we moved in here. Or at least a foam topping . . . He's still awake. Going to bed so early, hard to sleep. Should I talk to him? No. . . . Wonder what happened with my mama's best comforter? Haven't thought about it in years. All blue-and-white squares. Did Aunt Ellen get it or did . . . How quickly everything gets scattered when you . . .

From the darkness Sam suddenly said, "I went through his desk this morning."

Mary said softly, "Did you?" She thought, how often it happens. I'm thinking something and he'll start talking about it.

"Six desk drawers. His whole life." The mattress sagged as he turned toward her. "Are we wrong? About the kids?"

"No. We were right," she said firmly.

He groped for the cigarettes on the night table. A match spluttered and the flame threw split-second gargoyles on the wall. She smelled the acrid fumes of the match as the cigarette end glowed.

He said, "The undertaker didn't think so."

"It wasn't his decision to make."

"He said it was a purifying experience, the soul already gone and now the – the body returning to the elements."

He felt her sudden shudder; he turned and his arm went over her. "I'm sorry, honey. I'm a little goofball today. You know."

Mary thought, yes, I know. But you don't know why I shivered. I remembered something. What Mark said this afternoon when I told him he and Shirley couldn't come along tomorrow. His big eyes staring at me. "You shouldn't deny us this experience, Mama." As if he were talking about one of his experiments. I won't tell you, Sam. But starting tomorrow those children are getting out of the house. To the park. To the playground. I'll take them there myself. The way he said it to me wasn't normal! She felt anger warming her. Of course he was normal! Just a child! With a child's normal curiosity! About all things!

She felt Sam sigh deeply, shudderingly. She said, "Sam?"

He did not answer, and she realized that he was weeping, silently, rackingly, in that stupid tradition that he would be less of a man if he opened his grief. . . .

The pneumatic-chested waitress saw Robin shiver. The woman said, "Honey, would you like to move to the next booth? You're right under the air-conditioner. No, they ain't turned the air-conditioners on yet. It must be a draft."

Reseated in another booth, after the waitress had gone, Bob Farrell smiled at Robin and said, "You've got a sensitive inner thermostat, haven't you?"

"Sensitive." That word again. Robin tried to smile. She lowered her eyes to the menu. There had been no cold air draft; she had been thinking of the Elias family and suddenly she had shuddered, violently, without volition. Now she felt strangely uneasy. Her grandmother's words came back to her. Robin, visiting, had suddenly shivered.

"Somebody walked on your grave," the old woman had said solemnly.

Robin shook herself inwardly. Her period had begun unexpectedly that afternoon, so she was depressed. It was all a matter of chemistry.

Then she thought, yes, if it was at all possible, she would visit Harriet Elias the next day. Or some day . . .

It turned out to be a very pleasant dinner; Bob Farrell openly appreciated the food; for her part she felt none of the usual on-date strain of making conversation. Bob enjoyed the food and let her enjoy hers. She had a quick thought – this is how it would be in a good marriage. Two people completely at ease. No pretentions. No postures. No stupid we-must-fill-the-emptiness jabberwock. Just the good of being together, of knowing love was there. . . .

She felt her face going red; oh, this curse of the blush, would her autonomic system never grow up? Thank heavens her date was tactful. He looked at her, smiled, but made no comment.

The meal over, Bob Farrell stopped at the delicatessen section on the way out and bought a bagful of bagels for himself and another one for her; in her bag he had the clerk put an assortment of the circular doughnut-holed rolls ranging from onion-flavor to sesame-seeded.

Then, in spite of her laughing protest, he had the clerk add a carton of cream cheese and a couple of pounds of thinly sliced smoked salmon.

"Bagel, cream cheese, and lox!" he told her. "The manna the Lord slipped the Israelites from heaven."

They had reached the top of the pass; an air view of the city was below them, a geometry of fixed and moving fireflies.

Bob said suddenly, exuberantly, "Aren't you just crazy about Southern California?"

He said it so boyishly that Robin wanted to laugh, touch his face, tell him, yes, yes, I like what you like!

Aloud she said carefully, "It's another cliché, but I miss the change of seasons."

He grinned at her. "I've got a standard answer for that. If you miss the spring rains, go stand in a shower until you get the sniffles. If you miss the fall season, get a couple of sacks full of leaves and chase them around a windy back yard with a rake for a couple of hours. If you miss shoveling the winter snow, climb in a deep-freeze and do a hundred push-ups!"

She laughed with him; again she found herself enjoying his exuberance, the white of his teeth in his deeply tanned face.

When they were driving on the Hollywood side of the hills again, he said, "Movie?"

She told him yes, if he wanted to go to one.

He said, "What I'd really like to do tonight is – " He shook his head ruefully. "Why is it that life is full of so *many* clichés?"

She told him that she supposed that was because most things had been said before.

"Not between us," he said.

She thought, he has such lovely, unmarred skin.

"I'd like so very much to have you come see some of my work. If that doesn't sound like a variation of 'Come up and see my etchings,' correct me."

Robin thought, he's so desperately shy! So wonderfully, boyishly shy! With that downcast look through long lashes. It was reminiscent of someone she had recently seen. Of course! Mark Elias! Bob Farrell's look, the adult counterpart of the boy's shy, downward glance when praises were cloying.

She smiled. She said, "I'd like very much to see your photographs."

She liked his quiet response. No forced jokes, no disclaimers of intent, no torrents of thankfulness. Just a simple "I'm glad."

Robin said, "How old are you?"

"Decrepit. Twenty-four last December."

He was older. Good.

He touched her hair. "Beautiful."

Robin felt her face go warm again.

He said, "How strange!" At her puzzled look: "You didn't say 'Thank you.' I like that. I think people who react to a compliment about their physical appearance with a 'Thank you' are presumptuous, don't you? After all, what have we to do with the genes that made my hair blond and yours like midnight?"

She told him she agreed with him about the accident of body. As she spoke, she thought, what a gentle look he has. Gentle. That word again. "Your gentle virtues," Tony Dumont had said.

Bob Farrell said, "When I was a cave dweller, there was a redheaded girl in the group who spent practically all of her waking hours brushing her hair." At her look: "Didn't I tell you about my cave dwelling?"

She told him that he hadn't.

"Oh, that was right after I got my army discharge," he told her. "Do you know about those Grecian caves?"

She shook her head.

"It's an island in the Aegean Sea. A whole cliff dotted with caves. Full of drop-outs. Mostly Americans."

"Living in caves?"

"Sure. They've got an international reputation. I heard about them in Saigon. Nirvana. The Establishment tries to find it at one hundred dollars a day in Vegas or Miami Beach. You can make it in the caves for a couple of dollars a week."

Robin said, "I've always wanted to do something like that."

"Why haven't you?"

"Lack of opportunity. Lack of something."

He smiled. "You just don't move in the right drop-out circles."

"Why did you come back?"

He said, "I had no more reason to stay there. It served its purpose. I meditated on my navel and found my answers."

"Would you tell me what they are."

He said, "I decided that I couldn't change history. So I might as well relax and enjoy. Here and now. And use whatever abilities I have."

"In photography?" she asked him.

He said, "No, commercially that's a nothing. Uni-dimensional. All still photography does is freeze the moment of an emotion. I want to make a larger, longer comment than one-twenty-fifth of a second. That means motion pictures. My own."

She asked him, "Isn't that terribly expensive?"

"Not the way I'd do it. One-man job. Documentaries that comment on the heroic non-heroes of our times."

She wondered how close he had been to that hairbrushing girl in the cave. . . .

He was saying, "I don't often do that. Lay my ambitious soul bare."

She told him she was glad he had. Then she added, "When do you start? Motion pictures."

He laughed shortly. "When I get the gelt. I need camera, tripod, sound equipment, and a bus to carry it around. The whole package." He smiled at her. "I'll get them."

"I'm sure you will," she told him.

She didn't quite expect to be driven up to one of Westwood's sparkling new mica-on-stucco luxury apartment houses. As Bob parked the car in the fluorescent brightness of the sub-garage, he appeared to sense her confusion. He grinned and said, "Honestly, I do!"

In the ascending elevator he explained quickly – an aunt had left him a small legacy; he had moved in here as an antidote to the scrubby places he had lived in since his arrival in California.

"Even if it only lasts a couple of months," he grinned, "it'll be worth it."

She found the apartment an absolute delight; masculine yet not self-consciously so. The walls were forest green and the furniture white naugahyde-covered, with the wall-to-wall carpeting a warm coral.

She said, "Did you have an interior decorator do this?"

He said, wide-eyed, "I'm the culprit. Is it that terrible?"

She told him she liked what she saw, and his obvious relief at her approval was so great that she found herself thinking that this, indeed, was the nicest boy she had met since she had left home.

He led her into the sunshine-yellow tiled kitchen. "Now I'll confess. I'm also a frustrated chef. This gadget really is why I took this apartment."

It was a device Robin had never seen before; an oven, powered by something Bob called a "magnetron tube," which sent out radar waves that cooked and fried and baked miraculously all in moments.

Bob demonstrated with stuffed clams that came icy out of the deep freeze and, after three minutes inside of that miracle box, sent up delicious odors.

Then he said, "As long as I've cooked them we might as well eat them. Go down the hall, turn left, and look at my etchings and I'll be along with the food in a minute."

She followed directions and found herself in a small room decorated with a divan, an inflated vinyl easy chair, a Lucite end table, and walls covered with photographs of all sizes and shapes.

She saw at a glance that the work was good – no, she quickly decided, some of them went beyond that word into superb. They were all of the city – old Los Angeles – with the contrast of affluence and ghetto poverty making its comment, in each frame, by soft-focus double printing of the arrogantly expensive civic buildings behind the sharp focus of the hovels of the ghetto poor.

She became so engrossed in the pictorial documents that Bob's entrance was a surprise. She turned to him and saw the artfully arranged tray, the stuffed clams in pastel bowls, the array of dips on the multicolored lazy Susan, the soft sheen of silverware, the linen white of napkins.

At her enthusiasm, he modestly disclaimed his contribution with: "Out of the deep freeze. All of it! My only contribution is a sprinkle of this and a sprinkle of that."

"It's the sprinkle that does it," she told him.

"How right you are!" he grinned. "Let's collaborate on a book of Best Sprinkles!"

Collaborate? The word momentarily took the fun away, but she quickly lost herself in the outrageous chapter headings Bob was suggesting, and as she listened, her eyes approved the golden nimbus of his hair, the beauty of his face . . . the movement of his lips. . . .

He suddenly said, "Oh, gosh! The coffee!"

She didn't want him to go, but she said nothing. He returned with a softly gleaming tray on which rested a small silver pot and two cups dancing with enameled butterflies.

She took her coffee in the embrace of the inflated chair; at her involuntary reaction at her first sip, he laughed ruefully. He said, "My cooking feet of clay! I'm still looking for that Swedish woman they used to have on television who straightened out coffee syndromes. Would you settle for a Coke?"

She said, "No, no, it's fine!" But it really was bitter.

He took a sip and stood up from the divan. "That's terrible! I'll dump the whole thing!"

"No, no, really! I like it strong." She was in such a state of sudden euphoria that she didn't want him to leave, she wanted him there, blond Sir Galahad with a radar range.

He touched a button and music began. Soft strings and violins, distant as a sunset. She listened to him talk of many things, and her eyes adored him.

After a few moments she forced herself to concentrate on his words. He was saying, ". . . the opportunity was never greater! With the television networks going into theatrical production and bringing the cliché of their television films to the theater, honesty, daring, originality will be at a premium. That's why I've got to get a stake together to set up my own producing company."

She suddenly felt terribly thirsty. Between the clams and the anchovy dip, no wonder, she thought.

She interrupted him in the midst of his, "Cameraman . . .

director . . . cutting . . . do them all . . . no union scale . . ."

"Bob, forgive me," she said. "Could I have some water?"

He said, "Of course!" But in a moment he was back full of apologies to tell her that he had completely forgotten – there had been a posted notice earlier that the water system would be turned off for repairs starting at ten o'clock that evening. He offered more of the coffee with: "This is really all I have!"

So she drank and drank once more.

Bob Farrell sat down on the floor near her chair and began to talk again, so boyishly, of his ambitions. She tried to listen, but it was very difficult.

She thought, I'm falling asleep, that's terrible, impolite, but I can't help it . . . my eyes . . . if I just close them for a moment he won't notice. . . .

After a little while Bob Farrell got to his feet. He rubbed his jaws. They ached from so much talking, but from past experience he had found that it was important to keep talking. What was the word – syngerism. The low, monotonous tones and the Seconal-loaded coffee; one interacted on the other until the eyelids shut.

He walked over to her and looked down. Eyelids shut all right. He snapped his fingers close to her face. Out like the proverbial light. Well, on with it! He removed her shoes and placed them carefully parallel to each other on the floor.

Mary Elias thought, it's the first time he's let me drive, when he was in the car, without an argument. Since we were married. I wish he *had* argued. He hasn't said a single word since we left. Nor has Dave. Or Harriet. I wish I knew what to say to them. I grieve, but how can my grief be as theirs? If only this morning the same furnace would burn up that terrible hate they have for her, burn it and be gone the way Nat . . . I must not think of that. Think normal thoughts. I want everything normal. But why does Dave look at me as if I were a fellow conspirator? I don't know whatever it is *you* know, Dave. I don't want to know. All I want is to get there, say good-bye to Nat, and get home and make lunch for the children. Just that. Nothing more.

Robin awoke. The first object that she saw was the familiar blue-green dial of her alarm clock with its inexorable pair of black hands.

She thought sleepily, clock's crazy. And then the next thought – I'm home – brought her sitting upright. Her mouth opened and a small squeal came forth. In her chair by the window! A man asleep!

She clutched the bedclothes up around her, then she realized that she was shoeless but fully clothed. In what she had been wearing the night before!

The sleeper snored softly. A dark head turned. She saw, unbelievably, that it was Tony Dumont.

She threw the covers aside and, all in one motion, was in front of him. "What are you doing here?" she cried.

His eyes had opened at the thump of her feet. He sat up. He blinked.

"Answer me!" she demanded. "What are you doing here?"

He said mildly, "I brought you home."

She moved closer to him, fury in a wrinkled yellow dress, her hair tumbled. "You'd better tell me! How did I get here? What happened to Bob Farrell?"

Tony Dumont unfolded from the chair. He looked down at her. He said, "He got occupied with other things. So I did the honors." He started for the door. "I'll be talking to you."

She was suddenly between him and the exit. "Oh, no, you don't! You tell me what happened! What were you doing at Bob's? Was I asleep? Why did he let you take me away? Why didn't I wake up? It's afternoon! Don't stand there like an idiot! Answer me!"

He sighed deeply. He said, "Okay. Mind if I sit down? You'd better, too."

He moved back and unhinged into the chair he had just left. He took out a pipe and matches and began to try for a light with excruciating slowness.

She finally exploded with: "How long do you think I am going to wait?"

He said, "I think you are going to wait until I tell you." He sucked on the pipe. For the first time she saw that the knuckles of both of his hands were cut, the deep scratches outlined with clotted blood.

He said, "A strange thing happened to me on the way to the studio last night. My ego began to ache. Since I've usually got a non-reacting ego, I stopped at a bar, took a stiff one, and inventoried. Why had you turned me down? My neck was clean, my nails were trimmed, I had shaved in the morning, my suedes were brushed, my pants had a built-in crease, and my jacket was pure cotton corduroy."

She said intensely, "I'm not finding you amusing!"

He said quickly, "Oh, I'm not trying to be amusing! Please let me tell you in my own way. It's the only way it's going to make sense. Now, please, sit down."

As she seated herself rigidly on the nearby footstool, he went on: "Where was I? Yeah. My ego. So I said to myself, who is this character, this paragon who's beating my time? Having been around, I've got all sorts of sources of information to check out about specific kings and cabbages. I made a few telephone calls. I got Mr. Farrell's address and got into my car and went looking for you."

Her hands were clasped tightly together. She said, "What right have you – "

He interrupted. He said, "Let's say that I have the same right as the woodsman who went after Little Red Riding Hood."

She was on her feet again. "Are you out of your mind?" Her eyes were on his skinned knuckles. "What did you do to Bob?" She turned quickly and started for the telephone.

He said sharply, "You'd better hear me out first!"

The new harshness of his voice made her turn.

He said, "I got the same information from a half-dozen sources. Mr. Farrell, to put it bluntly, is a small-time operator in posed pornography."

She looked at him blankly.

He said, "I said 'small time.' That is to say his output is small, but he gets the top prices for his original prints. Because the meat is fresh."

She said softly, "Are you out of your mind?"

He looked at his pipe. "So I went there and got you. And

brought you home. And put you to bed. I apologize for spending the night here. I sat down just for a moment to make sure you were all right and fell asleep myself. It *was* rather late."

She said slowly, "You hit him!"

His knuckles flexed.

A vagary of cold air drifted upward and touched nakedness. Panic screamed through her.

At the look on her face he said quickly, "What's the matter?"

She tried to speak, but her throat constricted. She managed to whisper, "Tell me!"

"I told you! As soon as I found out what kind of an insect Mr. Farrell was, I went looking for him and for you." He smiled. "A slightly shopworn Lancelot in a beat-up station wagon."

She thought, there must be more to it! My underpants! I was wearing them! Now I'm without pants. That's corny, that's stupid, oh, my God, what happened? She reached sensorily, in renewed panic, for some feeling, an ache, moisture. But there was nothing!

Then, again, horror paralyzed her. The pad! She had been wearing one! Dear God, she had been overtired, had fallen asleep, and this monster had beaten Bob, kidnapped her, had raped – but, she felt nothing! Nothing! Surely if – She looked up at the face of him, the hard planes, the cruel stubble of beard. But he couldn't have – no one would have been so filthy! And if he had, would she get pregnant? She didn't know! Oh, God, there was so much she didn't know!

Looking down at her stricken face, Tony said to himself, what the hell am I protecting her for? She thinks I'm a big bad bully who beat up her date in a jealous rage. It's about time she lost her pink balloon.

Aloud, he said, "Sit down. I'll tell you the rest of it."

Wide eyes radar-fixed on him, she sagged down on the closest chair.

He said, "With your naïve approach to life, I don't understand how you stayed a virgin this long!"

Virgin? How did he know?

He went on. "There is an inexorable law of averages, and sooner or later it catches up even with wide-eyed pink-and-white innocents. It caught up with you last night."

Last night?

"I pulled the old 'I've got a telegram for you' gambit. When he opened the door, I crashed in. You were lying on the sofa."

Sofa?

"You were completely dressed."

Completely? No. How could I be? Where –

"At first I thought you were asleep or had passed out. Mr. Farrell was full of righteous anger. The girl had had one too many and had passed out and he was letting her sleep it off."

But only coffee!

"But I couldn't reconcile the reports I'd had on him with his big, blue-eyed protestations of innocence. I looked around. He didn't like it. I convinced him to cooperate. I continued to look around. He had a dark room. He still might have gotten away with it, but, as a cameraman, he's an eager beaver. He'd already started to develop."

Develop? Develop what?

Tony Dumont reached into his pocket and took out two small, tightly rolled films. He unreeled one of them and held it to the light. He said, "This reel was undeveloped, but I exposed it to the light so it's all black." He threw the exposed, opaque film on the table. He unrolled the second film. "This is the one – the negative he'd already developed." He handed it over to her. When she did not respond, he put the film alongside the first spool. Without looking at her he walked toward the door. "My only suggestion is that if you're going to date out-of-the-wood-work type photographers, make sure they don't drop a sedative in your demitasse." Without looking at her, he left, closing the door emphatically.

Robin stood there for a moment, her eyes fixed on the strips of acetate. She moved slowly toward them. She picked up a roll. The surface of the film was blackened. She put the roll down and picked up the second one. Her fingers closed on the edge of one of the frames and when she lifted the roll off the table, the film uncoiled of its own weight so that it hung like a thin snake. She held the strip up toward the morning sunlight; when she brought the small frame into focus, she cried out, and the film fell from her fingers to the floor. She stooped and picked the roll up again. She ran to the window and held the strip to the glass. There were many frames, and she was in each one of them, alone in each of them, silver black in negative, starring in each of them, positioned on her face, on her back, on her side, the lens peering sharply, ruthlessly, past breast, through up-thrust legs, exploring, leering. And where her face appeared, it was the eyes-closed glistening look of post-ecstasy satiation.

She was crying so heavily now that she did not hear the door open; it was not until the man spoke that she turned and saw him.

Tony Dumont said, "I forgot to tell you one thing. You don't have to worry about having been raped. Mr. Farrell is quite incapable. He cannot be aroused by anything but boys." Then, almost as an afterthought, he added, "I didn't either. That's not to say I wasn't tempted." He went, closing the door behind him.

Robin Shepherd groped her way to her bed and threw herself on it face downward and wept. In relief, and in shock, and for the splintered face of the boy with blue eyes and a blond nimbus.

Chapter 7

It was the night of the day of Nat Elias's cremation; they sat in the living room of Sam and Mary's apartment, all of them except the children who had been put to sleep across the way.

That had been Sam's thought; why expose the children to the family's unhappiness? It was good for the adults to get together, to find strength in each other, but not for the youngsters.

Mary had agreed, and after supper she had brought the children to the other apartment; she had tucked Shirley away in Harriet's bed, then had decided that it wouldn't be right to put Mark into his late uncle's bed, so she made up another bed on the living room sofa for the boy to use whenever he got weary. From the looks of the pile of books he had brought along to read, it was obvious that he would be up until all hours, but this night, of all nights, his mother decided, it made little difference. Anyway, all she had to do was pop across the hall to see that all was well.

So now the adult survivors of the Elias circle sat quietly in the apartment across the way – Sam, and Mary, and Dave, and Harriet, and her suitor, Max Alt. The latter had asked to come, and Sam had agreed that it would be a good thing for Harriet.

Sam had put a carafe of wine on the table. Other than Dave no one had drunk, and he was now on his fourth tumblerful, Sam noted. He watched concernedly as his younger brother held the glass to a lamp shade so that the light, shining through the red liquid, beamed on the white carpet.

"Blood," the man muttered.

Sam said, "Dave!"

Dave said thickly, "Well, what's wrong with saying 'blood'? Since when is that an undesirable word?" He looked around at the circle of eyes on him. "Somebody tell me – is there anything wrong with the word 'blood'?"

Mary said soothingly, "Of course not. It's a very descriptive word."

Sam was looking at the carpet. He said, "Just like in the movies." All eyes went to him. "I mean this morning. The rain. On our way home. In the movies it always rains at funerals. Everybody standing around under umbrellas."

Mr. Alt said, "I hope Harriet didn't catch a cold. This time of year."

Mary said, "Are you all right, Harriet?"

Harriet nodded. Everyone looked at her concernedly; all through the misery of the hours since Nat had died, she had been without words, without tears.

Sam looked up in time to see his brother refilling the glass. He said, "The cookies are very nice, Dave. You haven't eaten."

Mary said, "Perhaps I'd better go look in on the children – "

Sam restrained her. "For heaven's sake, you were in there no more than five minutes ago. Let them alone!"

Mary said, "You're right." She sighed deeply. The character of the sigh suddenly reminded her of her Aunt Daphne, so long forgotten, the widowed one, who, with the loss of her husband, had gained a deep, reverberating sigh for every and all occasions. It had become a small family joke: "Aunt Daphne's got a sigh for everything from a fallen cake to a World War."

And this night, Mary thought, I've inherited long-ago-dead Aunt Daphne's one distinction. . . .

Sam thought, oh, my God, how can I go down to the office tomorrow without Nat? How can I handle it? I haven't had time to learn! Is heart disease hereditary? Will I die like that – choking for a breath?

Dave thought of the flame that morning. He alone had watched it rise and fall, the small burning that had been a life, now, beyond the mica window, a flow of incandescence downward. . . .

Harriet sat there with the thought she had clutched for hours – to keep her mind an emptiness, a receptacle of nothing, spilling no memories, shut tightly against the horrors that clamored to climb into her head.

Max Alt thought, my arthritis is hurting. Every bone. I've got to get home, put a hot compress. . . . They're all so sad, so quiet. . . . What a tragedy. . . . Poor Harriet. Such a wonderful person. First chance I get, I'll apologize about the trip. Such a fine, clean woman deserves respect. Well, I think I've sat here long enough. . . . It wouldn't be impolite. . . .

He got to his feet, "I hope everybody will excuse me, but I've got appointments in the morning. Not that they're more important – "

Mary saw the man to the door; when she returned she saw that Sam was talking earnestly to his brother. From what she overheard, she realized that her husband was trying to get the silent Dave to come down to the office the next day to help him with the maze of problems with which Nat's death had left him.

Mary moved over to Harriet. She said, "Harriet, I've got an idea. Why don't you stay here tonight? I'll get the children now and you could sleep with Shirley. It's such a big bed. You'll be very comfortable." When the other woman did not respond, Mary reached down and took her elbow, and Harriet got to her feet docilely. "Come on, you must be very tired."

Sam called out after them, "Hey, where you two going?"

Mary told him that Harriet was staying overnight with them, and Sam agreed that was a good idea.

Dave reached for the wine.

In a few moments Mary came back into the room. She said, "I'm going over to get the children. It's their bedtime."

Sam said, "Okay." He turned to his brother. "It'll only be for a coupla weeks, Dave. I mean, you could get someone to write down the lectures or you could go nights to make up the time, couldn't you? I mean, after all – "

Dave Elias heard none of it. He tilted the glass and let the warm, soothing sacramental wine flow down his throat.

When she awoke that morning, Robin remembered crying in her sleep. She had no memory of why she had cried, only that somewhere in the dark of slumber she had wept and wept. She recalled having read somewhere that dreaming was a catharsis; she took a deep, shuddering breath, got out of bed, pulled her nightgown over her head, and began to do her five minutes of Canadian Air Force exercises. When they were over, as she stood there deep-breathing, she caught a glimpse of her nakedness in the dresser mirror and suddenly memory exploded in her. She cried out, rushed into the bathroom, hurriedly soaked a towel with cold water and held the wet of the cloth to her face.

When she felt better, she put on a robe and went to her telephone directory and looked up a number.

"Is Mr. Morgan there? . . . Oh, hello, Mr. Morgan, this is Robin. I'm . . . fine. . . . It's just that it's early in the morning. . . . Mr. Morgan, tell me something – please – whom do I go see to get into the morgue? . . . *Your* morgue. I'm writing an article and I need some background material. . . . Oh, that's great! I'll go right over. Thank you."

Mary thought, times like this I wish I were Catholic. The priest comes over, he's an older man, he knows what to say, he's said it so many times. I'm a foolish woman. What could a priest say to her? Or a minister, or a rabbi? She'd lived in a home without God all her life, heaven help her – you've got to start believing when you're very young. Dave was right. Mark has to have religious training. Shirley, too. Then, when they lose Sam and me, they'll have some kind of faith to help them until the shock wears off. It could happen to Sam and me all at once while they're still children. . . . Poor Harriet. She knows it's morning, but she doesn't want it to be. Nat was her strength and she was Nat's. All their lives. Sam said so. If I could help her, say the right words. But I've never been good with words. Not even with my own children. Sam doesn't expect words from me. We speak to each other with our lives. But I'll have to find words soon for Mark. Did he really tell the truth when he said Grandma told him to play that tape? Sam doesn't think so. I read somewhere children have a cruel sense of humor. But it can't be that. Mark never makes jokes. . . . I must talk to him about Nat's death. He must never blame himself. The doctor said it could have happened any time, anywhere. All the children wanted to do was give us entertainment. There is no sin in that. . . . So late – I'd better try to get her up. . . . Harriet! Wouldn't you like some breakfast? Shirley is waiting to eat with you. She loves you so very much. And Mark, too. Harriet, I want you to think of the children. Nat had a full life, but the children are just starting theirs. Think of Shirley and Mark, Harriet. They need your love so very much. . . . Oh, yes, yes, cry, cry! No, no, I'll hold you, no one will come in, you've held your tears too long! Cry, Harriet, and it'll be the way my own mother said – the tears will reach to heaven and make flowers grow on his pathway to God.

Robin Shepherd sat in a room of *The Los Angeles Times* at a long table on which an attendant had just piled a stack of newspapers. She quickly scanned the front page of the first paper, then began to turn pages.

She found what she was looking for in the fifteenth paper she'd examined. It was not on the front page, but on an inner page of a regional section. The headline read: "POLICE PUZZLED BY SANTA MONICA MURDER."

In the terse language of newspaperese, she read the facts: At midnight, the night before, a strolling couple had found a man, obviously badly hurt, writhing in the moonlight along the beach. Police had been called, and the man had been taken to the emergency room of a local hospital. There it had been determined that he had been mutilated in unprintable ways. The man had died shortly after admission. From the nature of the wounds, the article went on, the police believed that the man had been the victim of either gangster vengeance or a jealous husband.

The following day's paper contained only a small item that the police were still looking for the "Mutilation Murderer."

It was not until she turned to the paper of seven days later that Robin found the next item. This one stated that the murder victim had been identified, as a result of a tattoo mark, as one Merle Lambert, aged thirty-two, assistant engineer on an oil tanker leased to one of the major oil companies.

Two days later, there was a double column spread on the front page:

POLICE ARREST SUSPECT IN MUTILATION MURDER
SANTA MONICA MATRON LINKED TO SAILOR KILLING

The fluorescent above the table began to hum like a hive of disturbed bees; Robin heard the sound vaguely; deep in concentration on the newsprint, she turned a startled face at the touch of a hand on her shoulder.

"Hi, Robin! Hey, I'm not Rock Hudson, but you don't have to look *that* startled!"

Robin said, "I'm sorry, Mr. Morgan, I was so immersed – "

"Immersed in what?" he demanded.

Robin started to close the paper but he caught the sheet and folded it back. "Now, now! Hey, this murder! I remember that. Psychotic grandma in Santa Monica who cut up her young lover for kicks. That it?"

Robin said lamely, "I – I met someone in the family."

The newspaperman wasn't listening. He was already turning a page. He said, "Yeah, yeah, that was quite a story! And quite a trial."

A communicator chime sounded and a wall speaker intoned. "Jim Morgan wanted in Editorial. Jim Morgan wanted in Editorial."

When the man had rushed off, Robin bent over the newspaper again.

"So I figured since it's just around the corner and I'm home all day anyway, we might as well get the facts – okay with you?"

"Yes, Papa," said Mark Elias dutifully.

"Well, what do you know, we got a green light! If we were driving it would be red, believe me." He laughed nervously as he stepped off the curb. "How do you like that! I started to take your hand! A college boy!"

"Not yet, Papa."

"No, not yet. Thank God, you still have a few years with me and Mama. And Shirley. Watch the curb!" He laughed shortly. "Shirley! You could think I was committing the crime of the century, taking you away without her. But I needed the expert, not his satellite!"

"Who are you buying this recorder for, Papa?" Mark asked, short legs pumping to keep up with the longer ones.

"Didn't I tell you? Well – uh – it's for this – uh – fellow that comes in my office. He got to talking he wanted to buy one of these cassette jobs and didn't know which kind to get. So I told him about my son, the expert. Well, here we are. Say, they got quite a window display! Every make, eh?"

"Yes, Papa."

"Say, I meant to ask you, this friend of mine is crazy about sound effects and animal sounds and all that stuff. Do they have that in cassettes?"

"I'm not quite sure," his son told him. "But any of that material can be transcribed to cassettes."

"That's good," his father told him. "This – uh – fellow is crazy about sounds. Particularly animal sounds. Do you ever shop in this place?"

"Occasionally," his son answered.

"I mean, do they have good animal sounds? Cows, dogs, cats?"

"I'm sure they have," Mark told him.

"Well, that's good news!" Sam Elias paused; he looked down at his son for the first time. "You do much shopping here, Mark? Oh, I asked you that already, didn't I?"

"Yes, Papa."

Fifteen minutes later, as the clerk hovered by, Sam Elias said, "Well, I think that does it! I got a good picture of the whole situation with cassettes."

Mark said, "Aren't you going to buy one for your friend?"

"Huh? Oh, no." Sam cleared his throat nervously. "I can tell him about it and tell him to come here. Hey, look what time it is! We'd better get going. Your mama and I have to go downtown on business." To the clerk: "Thanks for your time, friend. I'll send in this – uh – fellow."

As they moved toward the door, father turned toward son. He said, "They've sure got a big stock. Is this where you got your cat sound?" At his son's look: "I mean the one you played at the party the other night. You know. The cat."

Mark said, without missing a stride, "No, Papa. I didn't."

"Then – uh – where did you buy it?"

"I got it from Grandma," the boy told him.

Sudden anger bunched Sam Elias's jaw muscles. With an effort he said nothing. He followed the small figure of his son out into the street.

"The minute I saw the pattern, I said this is for Shirley," Mary Elias said, "Do you really like it, darling?"

"Yes, Mama."

"Now you stop looking at that door. They won't be back for an hour. Anyway, when women are fixing dresses, it's no-man's-land, including brothers. Now stand straight."

"Yes, Mama."

"I think we'll have to take it up both in the front and in the back." As she began to pin up the dress, Mary thought, she's so small, she's still like a little doll. This cross-examination business – I don't like it, but Sam insisted. "Don't fidget. I'll stick pins in you. And you'd make a funny pin-cushion."

Shirley exclaimed, "I think they've come back!"

Her mother said sharply, "No, they've not come back! Do you think they flew to the store?" She softened her tone. "Anyway, by the time Mark explains all those recorders and things to your father, we won't even be halfway through with our dress-making." She took a deep breath and let it out before she spoke again. "Do you know someone who would have liked this dress? Grandmother. Remember how she always liked bright colors? Red?"

"Uh-huh," said Shirley.

"Yes, this is definitely grandmother's color. I miss her, don't you?"

"Yes – no, Mama."

"What do you mean, yes – no?" Mary said. "Now stop fidgeting! Of course you miss your grandmother!"

Shirley took a small, hidden, calming breath and then she said, "No, Mama."

"Well! I *am* surprised! Didn't you always have a good time when you played over at her house?"

Shirley said indifferently, "Sometimes."

"The way you and Mark always were eager to go over there," her mother stated. She shook her head. "Why didn't you have fun sometimes?" She made no more pretense of working on the dress. She kneeled facing her daughter. "Tell me!"

"Because."

"Because of what? Something she said? The games she played with you? The people you met there? The food you ate?"

Shirley said quickly, "Yes, Mama, that was it."

"What was it?"

"The food," the small girl said loudly. "Sometimes it was terrible."

"But Grandmother was a marvelous cook," Mary said. "When she wanted to be. At least every time I ate there. What in the world food didn't you like?"

Shirley thought for split seconds. Then she said, her eyes on the closed door, "Hot dogs. We had bad hot dogs."

"Oh, come on! I don't recall any climactic bellyaches! Are you having fun with me?" She waited, but her small daughter remained silent. "Well, at least I know one thing. You must have had fun playing those games." Small face lifted. "Like the time you made that tape recording of her cat."

For the first time Shirley's face grew animated. "Oh, yes!"

Mary Elias said, "Now really!" She forced a smile. "You *are* making a joke, aren't you?" Shirley's face was blank again. "You know mighty well Grandmother's cat wasn't even alive when you and Mark were there. I believe that cat died before you were born! Yes! Now you tell me the truth, young lady.

When did Mark record that cat sound to have fun with us at the party?"

Again the small girl's eyes were fused on the closed door.

"Now you can see I'm not angry with you, Shirley," Mary went on. "I just want you to tell me the truth. When did Mark put that cat sound on the tape? The afternoon of the party when you and he were in his room for all those hours? . . . Really, Shirley, I want an answer! A simple, courteous answer!"

A door sounded distantly.

Shirley leaped off the chair on which she had been standing.

"Shirley, you stay – "

"Mark's back!" She was already through the door, the un-hemmed rear of the new dress billowing with the speed of her going.

Robin sat white-faced before the spread of newsprint. Half an hour before she had asked for a new group of papers out of the file dated four years later than the ones she had been reading. She had found the item front-paged in the third one of the new group. It stated that one Arnold Elias, aged sixty-three, head of the Friendly Toy Company, had committed suicide, early the evening before, by dousing himself with gasoline, lighting the fluid, and then falling from the topmost floor of the Richfield Building in a screaming, flaming parabola. Motive unknown. Mr. Elias had been a prosperous, happy husband, the widow had informed the authorities.

The later editions noted that said widow had been acquitted of murder, a few years before, in the sensational Mutilation Case.

The story went on to list the suicide's children: Nat, Dave, Sam, and a daughter Harriet.

A short time later Robin left the newspaper building. Smog had descended on Central Los Angeles; it drifted in brown streaks through the high-rise canyons.

"Hello, Robin!" It was someone she had known in the newspaper's advertising department. She mumbled greetings and the man moved on with, "Smog's terrible, isn't it? You'd better get out of it. You look as if it's getting to you."

Robin moved away to the parking lot; she fumbled her way

into her car and started it, and when she handed her parking ticket and coins to the parking attendant, he called after her, but she kept on driving. A pulse beat in her forehead. The children! How horrible for the children! But perhaps they had been too young to understand. The small girl – what was her name? – Shirley – she would have been only two or three. But Mark would have been seven. How much one felt when one was seven! And the subconscious carry-over into the later years!

What stupidity of the police to have accused Grandmother Elias! And the district attorney compounding that stupidity with that trial! Dragging those kind, simple people through such horrors! All that trauma had undoubtedly led to the father's mental breakdown.

The defense attorney had been right; it had been a sadistic, drunken, teen-age gang roaming the beaches looking for excitement.

And that equally sadistic Mr. Dumont looking for his own brand of sensationalism and thinking she would join him in writing such lies! What superlative cruelty that would be, to subject that family to a renewal of the ordeal which, to them, must be a raw wound that had happened only a handful of yesterdays!

Thinking of Tony Dumont, she recalled the strip of film. She would never see him again! Never! She would always be grateful to him, but to look into his face after what he had seen of her . . .

She suddenly realized that she was on the Santa Monica Freeway; she had been driving automatically without consciousness of direction. She decided to continue on to the Coast Highway; she would turn there and then back onto Wilshire Boulevard and visit the Eliases. The rough draft of her article was in her handbag; before she polished it, she would read it to them, give them the assurance that she, at least, had done and would do nothing to hurt them further.

Misting rain began to fall; she turned on the windshield wipers and they began their busy, hypnotic beat.

Robin thought, it's really foolish, my going there. Airless, overheated place. . . . She took a deep breath. Nonsense! She pressed harder on the accelerator.

The door opened reluctantly an inch and a half. Below the brass inner chain Robin saw the blond gleam.

She said, "Good morning, Shirley. Is your mother home? You remember me – I'm Robin Shepherd. I was here the other night. To do a story about your brother."

Metal slid along a groove, link chain fell, and the door opened wide. Robin saw that heavenly smile again, heard the small, sweet greeting, "Hello, Miss Shepherd. Won't you come in, please?"

"Thank you, Shirley."

The hallway was dark, but beyond she could see the rain clouding the windows of the living room. She put her wet coat down as a small hand tugged at hers.

"Come on, come on!"

"Thank you." What a darling child!

In the living room, Shirley led her to the sofa and said, "Won't you please sit down, Miss Shepherd?"

Robin said her thanks and seated herself. She thought, how cool the air is! So unlike that other night. She looked around. It really was a marvelous room. Like a mountain aerie.

Shirley had dragged up a footstool and was now seating herself on it, wiggling for a comfortable position, then folding her hands in her lap and looking up brightly at her visitor.

Robin said, "Won't you please tell your mother I'm here?"

Shirley said, "Mama isn't here."

"Oh! Your father?"

"He isn't here either." Small eyes stared fixedly, mouth smiled pleasantly.

Robin said, "Oh!" She stood up. She said, "In that case, I'll come back some other time." Then she added. "Are you here all alone?"

The small blond head swiveled negatively.

"Oh! Is it your Aunt Harriet? I would like to talk to her."

Shirley turned. Her mouth opened. An amazing volume of voice shrilled: "Mark! Company!"

Then the small head turned and she looked back at Robin and smiled reassuringly.

Robin said, "So Mark is here. Good. I want to talk to him, too."

Shirley said conversationally, "He's coming. You can't hear it 'count of the deep acrylic carpeting. Wall-to-wall."

Robin repressed a smile. "I see."

Mark Elias entered the room. As he came toward her, Robin thought, how erect he walks. But then he does everything well. She said, "Well, hello!"

He gave her a vigorous handshake. "Good morning, Miss Shepherd. How nice of you to visit us."

"Thank you," she answered. "Are you and your sister quite alone?"

"Yes, ma'am," he said. "Would you like a Coke or a Tab? A Tab is the same as a Coke except that it uses calcium cyclamate instead of sugar. If calcium cyclamate is contradicted in your diet, I suggest a cup of tea."

Robin said, "Thank you very much, but I don't want a drink. But don't let me stop you or Shirley."

The boy said, "I'm not drinking."

Shirley said, "I'm bloated."

Robin again repressed a smile reflex. She said, "Really? Then I don't think you should." The rain had freshened; it sluiced over the huge windows. "This is a very wonderful room. It's like being on a ship at sea."

Mark had pulled up the matching footstool to the one his sister was on. He sat on it in the identical position Shirley had taken, with legs crossed, hands clasped in lap. He said, "I've never been on a ship at sea."

Robin said, "I'm sure you will. Someday."

He said, "Perhaps. If there's time."

Robin thought, you'll have time. It's all yours. If you were mine . . . her heart turned in her; she said quickly, "When do you think your mother will be home?"

Mark said, "Not for some time."

"For hours and hours," Shirley amended.

Robin thought, leaving small children alone in such a huge place for hours and hours! But then, she told herself, they're not quite just small children. At least not this beautiful boy. His dark, confident eyes. . . .

She said, "Your spring vacation will soon be over, won't it?"

Small heads nodded.

Wind crashed rain against the glass close behind her.

She said, "How are your experiments coming along?"

Mark said, "Which ones?"

"I mean in general."

He considered that, then he said: "In general quite well."

"That's good." She thought, now that was a brilliant comment! Aloud she said, "Do you mind if I ask you some more questions?"

The boy said, "No, ma'am."

Robin said, "Perhaps I ought to ask your mother's permission. Has she gone anywhere I could reach her by phone?"

Shirley yawned, then covered her mouth with her hand and said hastily, "Excuse me." Then she said, "She's gone to the funeral."

Again a gust of wind, and for a split second Robin thought that the building had swayed. But that was nonsense! This firm cylinder of stone and steel! Funeral? Had Shirley said that? But Nat Elias must have been buried days ago!

She saw that the small boy was frowning. She said, "Oh, I'm sorry. I mean, that someone's . . . passed away. Was it anyone close to the family?"

Shirley nodded her head affirmatively.

Robin looked at the boy. He said nothing.

Shirley said, "It was our Aunt Harriet."

Aunt Harriet? Had she heard correctly? The tall one, the spinster, the whisperer at the window?

She heard herself saying loudly, "You mean your aunt – the one who lived next door – the one I met – "

Shirley said, "Yes, ma'am."

Robin said, "Oh, I'm so sorry! It must have been sudden! What was it?"

Shirley looked at her brother. Mark said, "She committed suicide."

The rain was thundering against the glass.

Shirley said, "She hung herself. In her closet."

The walls moved and the floor was a wave. Distantly Robin heard the small girl's voice saying, "They said we were too young to go to the funeral."

And then the boy's distant voice, "The funeral had to be at once. It's part of the tenets of their religion."

How strange that the windows moved inward and outward like breathing ribs of a great creature! She heard her own distant voice: "Could I please have a glass of water."

Shirley's voice, close, soothing: "Lie back, Miss Shepherd. Just lie back. . . ."

No, no, she was better. A cold glass was put in her hand. She drank gratefully and the room was firm, locked in its stalwart walls. She looked at the hovering little faces, and she thought, I'm a poor example of an adult. Their own aunt and they're already adjusted, and, as usual, I fall apart at the inevitable fact of death.

She took a deep breath. They were young . . . enough of death. She tried to put vigor in her voice as she said, "I came here because I've finished my article about your winning the award. Would you like to read it? But perhaps this isn't the time." She added nervously, "It's only a rough draft, if you know what I mean."

The boy said, "Yes, ma'am. It's a preliminary version of what you intend to do as a finished product."

She looked at him carefully, but he was obviously very sincere. She unzipped the leather envelope she had brought with her, took out the manuscript and handed it to the boy. He took the papers, moved over to a light, and began to read.

She said, "If anything isn't clear, I'll be glad to explain."

Almost in that moment he moved back to her and returned the stapled sheets.

She looked her amazement. "Don't you want to read it all?"

He said, "I have, Miss Shepherd."

She realized that he must read in that new rapid manner. She said, "You read by scanning?"

He said, "Yes, ma'am. In a manner of speaking."

She waited for his critique, but he said nothing, just sat there looking at her. She said uncomfortably, "Well, what do you think?"

He said, "It's factual."

She said, "I should hope so!"

So dark in the room. Those small lifted faces, those luminous eyes. What could she say to them now? How could she comfort them? No, she need say nothing. Not to these wonderful children. They were all right. Quite all right.

She got to her feet. She said, "I really must be going."

Shirley said, "We'll see you to the door."

The boy said, "It was nice of you to call on us." He hesitated, then he added, "And, please, Miss Shepherd, about our Aunt Harriet. Mama and Papa told everybody not to call up or send flowers or condolences. Just remember her kindly."

Robin said softly, "I understand."

As she waited for the elevator, Robin thought of the wonder of mothering such cherubim.

Mark Elias stood in front of his sister. He said firmly, "You shouldn't have said that."

Her eyes were downcast. "I'm sorry."

"Anyway, not about the closet." He sighed, "Well, we'll just have to go there tonight."

She looked up eagerly, but he had moved away. He stretched out on the couch. He put out a hand, took up the magazine on the end table, turned pages, and began to read.

When Shirley came up to him, he kept on reading. She pulled at his arm. He looked at her.

"Let's play Grandma's game," she said.

He said, "Uh-uh. Wanna read."

"Please, Mark. *Please!*"

He said, "Okay!" He swung off the sofa. "I'd better go double-lock the door."

As he moved out of the room, she began to take off her dress.

Chapter 8

Mary Elias thought, he's aged. In these few days. New lines. Forehead. Under his eyes. Oh, my poor darling!

Sam Elias pounded the horn suddenly. He yelled angrily, "Look where you're going!"

Mary plucked at the safety belt. She said lightly, "When we get home, I think I'll do my famous striptease that slayed the girls back in P.S. 102."

Sam said somberly, "Let's face it! I'm a lousy father!"

"Now, Sam –"

"No, this time you're not going to shut me off! Am I a grown man? Have I had a fair education, everything considered? Can I talk to people normally without having them run to a Berlitz School? All right! Then something's got to be wrong with me that I can't communicate with my own kid! Somewhere, somehow, I do something wrong! And you're not going to tell me differently! Well? Aren't you going to answer me?"

Mary said, "When the general tells me not to talk, I obey orders." At his groan, she said, "All right, all right, I *have* got an answer. It isn't my own answer. I heard it on television the other morning." At Sam's repeated groan: "No, it wasn't one of those women on a talk show. It was a professor of psychology at one of the universities. I can't remember which one. Anyway, he said that this generation of parents is full of worry and guilt because they can't communicate with their children."

Sam said, "So what was *I* talking about? Ham sandwiches?"

"He said that, from his observations, in most cases the parents were beating themselves needlessly. Because the trouble, in most cases, was with the children."

"Now that's a bright statement! I'm in my forties and Mark's not quite thirteen, and he's to blame because I haven't intelligence enough to know how to talk to him!"

Mary said, "Sam, you've got to be patient. You can't pick out words – you've got to let me finish telling you what the man said."

"Ten to one he's an unmarried fruit!"

Mary said, "Whatever he was, he made sense. He said the trouble was the television."

Sam snorted. "Now that's an original answer!"

Mary plodded: "He said that by the time they're sixteen or seventeen, the average American child has spent twenty-two thousand hours watching television."

Sam looked his exasperation. "What the hell has television got to do with me not being able to talk to him?"

"I'm trying to tell you! Before television, those children would have been outside playing games with each other, talking, fighting – in other words communicating. Instead, they sit in front of the television set. So they don't know how to communicate. With their friends, with their teachers, their parents, or anybody else!"

Sam said, "Oh, that's a beautiful theory! There's only one thing wrong with it! Do you want me to tell you what's wrong with it?"

Mary waited patiently.

"What's wrong," he went on, "is that we've got an exception to the statistics! Mark doesn't watch television! Maybe an hour a week when there's something special on. Am I right or am I right?"

Mary had to admit that he was right. She thought, it's actually less than an hour a week. The glass in the front gathers dust.

She reassured him, "In a few years, no matter what, you'll communicate with each other. Wait and see."

Sam guided the car toward an off-ramp. He said, "I don't think so. With Shirley, maybe. But with Mark, I don't know."

Mary said, "What do you mean, you don't know! He's a good boy! When he gets older he'll talk to you!" She spoke so vehemently that Sam turned and looked at her in amazement.

"You just get me so mad, all of you, acting as if he were a freak or something!" she said defensively. "Would you rather have a stupid child with a big mouth?"

Sam grinned. "Okay, relax, tiger." He applied the brakes at the stoplight.

"Well, would you?" she demanded.

"I don't know," he said seriously.

She looked up at him in amazement. "You want a stupid child?"

"Not particularly," he told her. Deep lines raked his forehead. "But I would like to have the sense of being his father once in a while. More and more, when he looks at me, I feel as if I were on the wrong planet."

Mary Elias looked grimly straight ahead through the windshield. She said, "Now you're the one who's being stupid."

"Thank you!"

She turned quickly toward him, and he saw that she was truly angry. She said, "I'm proud that I'm the mother of a genius! Yes, a *genius!* And the fact that his sister adores him is good and healthy and I'm happy about that, too! And if you can't communicate with him – well, I can! With love and understanding and – and anything else it takes!"

As the car moved away from the parking lot, Max Alt said, "I should apologize."

The fluorescent street lights were occasional horizontal candles in the misted darkness; Harriet looked at Max and saw that he was frowning. Her pulse beat faster. She thought trouble, I don't want any more trouble!

He went on: "I swear to you I had no idea it was that kind of a movie."

She began to breathe again. She said, "It's all right."

Max Alt said emphatically, "It's not all right! They've got no right to show such things in a theater belonging to a chain where respectable people go! Believe me, tomorrow at the office, I'll write a letter to their corporation – the paper will burn!"

Harriet thought, Max, dear Max!

"Two and a half dollars a ticket! You heard what I said to that manager. Manager! Mr. Put-butter-on-the-popcorn! You know me, Harriet, I'm not one of those people who think that movies today should still be Nelson Eddy holding Jeanette MacDonald, although, believe me, they were plenty entertaining for the money! But unmarried people taking a bath together with only the soap bubbles covering! Well, I knew this was not something you wanted to see for an evening's entertainment."

Harriet thought, oh, Max, Max! She said softly, "I'm glad we left."

Max Alt said, "Even if I was alone, believe me I would have been uncomfortable. The whole story – that boy kissing the boy – " He made a spitting sound as his left foot clicked the high-low beam switch to warn an oncoming car that the lights were blinding. "When you agreed to forget everything for a couple of hours, believe me, I was proud of you. Now I'm ashamed. To take you to such – you'll pardon the word – entertainment!"

Harriet said softly, "No harm. . . ."

Max said, "Well, it's early. I'll get you home, you'll get a good rest tonight. I know you'll excuse me talking about this, but it's very apropos. Years ago, before my wife got her final sickness, when we were in New York we used to go to all the shows on Broadway, and she was just like you are when there'd be something, how should I say it, distasteful on the stage. She'd close her eyes. Tonight, when that, you'll excuse the expression, prostitute began with that young boy, I looked at you and you had your eyes closed. That's when I decided that enough was enough, even if we didn't get our money back." His free hand closed on hers. "You're a wonderful person, Harriet, and I thank God that I met you, and for entertainment we don't need what belongs in, you'll excuse the expression, in one of those houses in Paris, or in Egypt, or wherever they have those places. Don't you agree with me?"

She said, "Yes, Max." Yes, yes, yes, Max! Anything you say, Max. If you want movies with everyone in halos, and corsets, and hobble-skirts, and chastity belts, I'm your girl, Max!

Late that evening, instead of her usual lukewarm shower, Robin filled the tub with very hot water. When it was up to level, it was so hot that she could get in only by slow degrees, permitting toes, feet, ankles, and legs in turn to become accustomed to the heat. Finally she was submerged; she lay outstretched, her body numb, impersonalized by the heat.

She looked down in the water and she thought of the revealing postures, and she was suddenly very angry – for the first time, truly angry. It was not so much the bits of film; she thought of them as mechanical things made through an inhuman lens. Rather, the concentration of her anger was the touching, his hands using her with insolent intimacy.

The water was very still and clear; in the warmth her nipples stood out strongly; she remembered that they had been that way in one of the pictures, and she wondered what he had done, as she slept, to excite them. Had his mouth . . .

No, Tony Dumont had vouched that the man was a deviate. But he was also a photographer trying to get the best out of his material. . . .

She began to think, what if I *had* been raped. What would I have done? Would I have gone to the police? A doctor? Which doctor? One of those emergency hospitals? Walked in and said, "I've just been raped, would you please quickly do whatever you have to do to keep me from bearing an unwanted child?"

Unwanted? She thought, would I ever unwant any child?

The bite of the heated water was all gone; it now lay in a sensuous blanket around her. Robin closed her eyes. Her hands had been resting out of the water on the satin-smooth rims of the tub. Now she let them fall into the water and her right hand came to rest on the soft mound of her pubic hair. She thought, I've never even done *that*. When the girls talked about "happy hands" at school, I didn't know what they were talking about.

What had Tony Dumont said? Yes, "Sooner or later the law of averages catches up even with wide-eyed innocents."

What did *I* get caught up by? A fairy with a Rollei!

The water was getting cold. She thought, is there something wrong with you, too, Miss Shepherd? What's your deviation? Or aren't you even normal enough to have a deviation?

She got out of the tub abruptly, toweled herself quickly, filling her mind, as she did so, with the thoughts of the weekend – a trip to the Pasadena Art Museum where they were doing a California Design exhibit.

She put on a robe; it was not until she was putting her hair up that she stopped disciplining her thoughts long enough to remember that Tony Dumont had said something else. "That's not to say I wasn't tempted." She closed her eyes and for the first time in her life Robin Shepherd thought what it would be like to have a man thrusting within her.

"Well," said Aunt Harriet, "this is an unexpected surprise!" She looked down at their sweet faces. "And I might say a very welcome one. I was busy having the blahs. Come in, come in!"

To find the children at her doorstep, so to speak, was, indeed, an event. Not that they weren't little darlings, but in all the months since her brothers had taken adjoining apartments, the children had come to her only when they had been brought over by Mary or Sam.

Now, here they were, bright and bushy-tailed. And just when she needed them. She had taken a Dexamyl after Max had gone, and that had lifted her far out of the deep canyon into which she had plunged the moment she was back in the apartment, but she had said no to the invitation to go to late evening services at the temple with her brother and Mary, and that had brought the pain of Nat back to her. So thank heavens for these visitors! She would be bright and cheery with them, the babies!

She brought the children into the living room, tightened the belt on her robe, and sat down on the couch and curled her legs under her. "Well, now, tell me, to what do I owe this great pleasure?"

They had sat down together, side by side, the children; how devoted they were to each other! What a lovely word, "devotion"!

Shirley spoke. "We just wanted to be with you, Aunt Harriet."

Harriet glowed; what a sweet, fragile child that was! Like a doll, a regular little doll! Aloud she said, "That's very nice. Say, did I hear someone go in and out of your apartment this afternoon while your mother was gone?"

"No, Aunt Harriet," Mark said firmly.

"Well, I was half asleep. Listen, how about something to eat? I'll make some of my super-special waffles!"

Mark spoke. "No, thank you, Aunt Harriet. We've already had our dinner."

She was on her feet: "I know, I know, but a few waffles!"

"No, Aunt Harriet," Mark told her. "It's unhealthy to stuff oneself."

Harriet reseated herself. "A truer word was never spoken. Well, now, and what did you do today? Climb a mountain? Deep-sea-dive for treasure?"

Shirley giggled. Mark smiled.

"Hey! I got a couple of smiles! Say, that boosts my rating! Maybe the sponsor will give me a renewal!"

The children reacted happily again and Aunt Harriet felt another warm glow. Perhaps, at last, she was reaching them. As an aunt. As a human being.

Not that they hadn't always been friendly. It was just that her dreams of being Auntie, when they had been babies, had never been realized. Fun at Disneyland, and long walks in the zoo, and all that. It had never happened. Yet.

She had to admit it wasn't all the children's fault, if at all. She, herself, had always been so troubled that she didn't blame the children for not warming up to her. Who can warm up to an iceberg?

She made a decision: no more sorrow! Not for Nat, not for anyone or anything! Enough of walking through life with her soul dragging. She'd be an optimist even if she had to take the green pills by the handful. Sorrow brought on sorrow – tragedy brought on tragedy – maybe laughing at life would make it laugh with you. Sure, see how even the little ones were reacting!

She said brightly, "Listen, I've got a bright idea! Why don't we go to Disneyland tomorrow, the three of us? I'll talk to your mother and we'll make a whole day of it. Okay?"

Such silence. Shirley staring at her brother and the boy obviously deep in thought. What a bright, bright look he has, she thought. None of our family ever before – what a blessing! Of course he was too absorbed in his experiments, that child. She would insist, yes, insist on that Disneyland day! All right, Mary and Sam might say it was too soon after the tragedy, but what did tragedy have to do with these blessed children?

Aloud she said, "Well, what's the difficulty? So forget Disneyland, we'll go roll hoops in Griffith Park or make snowmen!"

Shirley giggled, "There's no snow!"

"She's making a joke," Mark told his sister.

"I like jokes," Shirley said. "Grandma used to make us lots of jokes."

Harriet Elias felt all joy drain out of her. She said, "Of course." She took a deep breath and let it out shudderingly. She said, "Children, tell me something."

Shirley said, "Yes, Aunt Harriet."

"I've always wondered. You spent so much time over at . . . Grandma's. What did you do?"

Shirley smiled.

Harriet said, "Now that's a complete answer." She turned to the boy. "Mark?"

He looked up at her. As always she felt the impact of those incredibly large eyes. She said, "Well?"

He said, "We played."

"That's reassuring," Harriet said. "You played."

"Yes, ma'am."

She told him that she was not "ma'am" – she was Aunt Harriet. She added, "Did the two of you just play or did you make friends with the neighboring children?"

Shirley smiled.

Mark said, "No, ma'am – uh, Aunt Harriet. Grandma played with us."

For a split second the woman was speechless and then she said, "Grandma played? That doesn't seem possible. Are you sure?"

Shirley nodded vigorously, and her brother said, "Yes, Aunt Harriet."

As the woman opened her mouth to speak, Shirley burst out enthusiastically, "Other people!"

Harriet Elias, at that moment, knew she should stop her inquiries. She knew it as definitely as anything she had known in her life, but her mouth opened, and air moved past her vocal cords, and she heard herself ask, "Were they grown-up people?"

Shirley looked at her brother. He nodded. Shirley said, "Oh, yes, Aunt Harriet."

The next words caught in the woman's throat, and then they came out: "What kind of games?"

Shirley smiled. She looked at her brother once more. The

small boy got up from his chair. He walked across the carpet to his aunt. A muscle began grasshoppering in her left cheek. He whispered in her ear. As she listened, it was as if he were injecting a drug with each word, bitter chemicals that grooved chasms in her face, thrust her eyeballs out, dropped her jaw slack so that her tongue hung out idiotically.

The boy stopped talking. He moved back to his chair and sat down again, hands in lap.

Aunt Harriet staggered to her feet. She swayed unsteadily. She turned, she rushed from the room. A door opened and the children listened to the sound of distant retching.

Mark Elias got to his feet. He said, "I'll go home now."

Shirley said, "Yes, Mark."

Mark said, "I'll tell Mama she asked you to stay."

Shirley smiled adoringly at her brother.

Some time during the night a sound tore Harriet out of sleep. Something was unfamiliar – the darkness itself – Oh, Nat, Nat! They burned you – no! Mustn't think of that! Water! Get some water! She sat up in the bed. She gasped. Something silhouetted against the window – what – oh! Shirley? Oh, yes, Shirley had stayed!

She felt quick nausea at the memory of the whispers. No, no, this was no time to think of that – the middle of the night – tomorrow she would think about it, clearly, unemotionally, decide whether to tell Sam and Mary, what to do to cleanse the filth put into that poor little innocent head. Wait a moment! What in the world was that child doing scrunched up on the windowseat this time of night?

Harriet got out of bed. She walked up to her niece. The small white oval of face lifted at her approach.

"Shirley, why aren't you in bed? What are you doing?" Small white rectangles on the dark wood. "Playing in *that* light?"

Shirley's smile was like dancing starlight. "Hi, Aunt Harriet! Did I wake you up? I dropped something."

"Well, I *was* sleeping, but I'm glad I woke up. Do you often do this – get out of bed in the middle of night?"

"I wanted to look at the writing," Shirley told her.

"Writing?" The woman groped out; a switch snapped and light flooded the windowseat and the row of papers. "What are they – "

"You can look at them if you want to," Shirley told her.

Aunt Harriet's hand went out to one of the rectangles. As she turned it over, she started to say, "What are – " then the words choked off abruptly. She lifted one of the papers close to her eyes; blood drained and suddenly it was a skeletal face staring through crucified eyes. Her voice, when she spoke, was tiny, choked, somewhere deep within her. "Where . . . did you find these?"

The small girl said quietly, "I didn't find them, Aunt Harriet."

The woman's fingers, with a will of their own, lifted the small pieces of paper one by one. Mama's handwriting . . .

"They're all about you, aren't they, Aunt Harriet?" Shirley said pleasantly.

Mama's scorecard. For a week, forty-five years ago. . . .

Small, persistent voices: "You had fifteen fathers, didn't you, Aunt Harriet?" She giggled. "Fifteen!"

The woman said, "Where . . . did you . . . get these?"

"Grandma."

"When?"

No answer.

"Are these all?"

"No, ma'am. Lots more."

"Where – "

"Mark sent them to him. Today. In a big envelope."

"Him?"

"Mr. Alt."

A very old woman turned away. The papers snowflaked to the carpet. She walked slowly out of the room.

Shirley carefully gathered up the scattered sheets. She climbed into her aunt's bed. She settled herself comfortably. She lay there listening.

"Good morning, Shirley!"

"Good morning, Mama."

"For heaven's sake, do you know your Aunt Harriet forgot to lock her door? Open all night! Where is she?"

"I don't know, Mama. I was sleeping."

Aunt Harriet, head bent in weariness, swayed on the pendulum of the living-room chandelier. Her reaching toes strained for the floor.

Part Three

Chapter 9

In the morning, after a phantom-filled night, as Robin left her apartment building, the craggy Mr. Dumont was there. He did not give her even a moment in which to feel the embarrassment she had anticipated; he grabbed her arm with an excited, "I was just coming up to see you! I've got some very important news! You didn't believe me about that family! Well, listen to this – the flash just came over the wire. Another of them is dead! The sister, Harriet Elias! Committed suicide!"

Robin started to tell him that she already knew about that, then she thought, what did he mean – "just came over the wire"? It had happened yesterday! The woman was already buried! Before she could speak, Tony turned and rushed down the steps toward the curb. Robin saw that his green station wagon was double-parked next to her VW and that a motorcycle policeman was just dismounting.

She thought, good, I'll get the officer to make him move the car before he writes the ticket, and then I'll drive off and be free of him.

She heard the policeman say, "Double parking's expensive on this street, mister!"

Then she heard Tony Dumont cry out "Charlie!" and the officer exclaimed, "Tony!" and it was old buddies' reunion at the curb.

The officer said, "How do you like that, I didn't recognize your car! How goes it, tiger?"

"Still foolin' them! How's Margaret?"

Robin leaned against her car and thought, this is too much. She stepped over and tapped the officer on the shoulder, and she said, "Is it illegal for me to drive my car away?"

The officer thought that was terribly amusing, and Tony introduced her to him; the lawman obviously liked girls and was feeling sociable, but the radio on his bike squawked a call and he took off.

"Get in my car," Tony told Robin. Then he grimaced. "Or your car. I'll tell you all about it."

"I know all about it," Robin told him. "If you'll excuse me – I really must – "

"Oh! I didn't know they had it on the morning news," Tony said. "Get in, anyway. I want to talk to you." When she did not answer, he added, "If I said please, I'd be begging, so don't expect me to say please."

He was so small-boy truculent that Robin wanted to smile for the first time since she had left the children the day before.

She said, "I was just going down to the drugstore. If you want to walk with me."

He looked at her with the usual amazed reaction she had experienced whenever she used the word "walk" in this town, but he recovered from the shock long enough to ask her to wait a moment until he moved his car and then he would join her.

Fifteen minutes later they were still walking, deep in argument, with the forgotten destination drugstore far behind them.

Tony said, "What's your implication? That the family was born under an ill-fated star? Aquarius was out of conjunction with Venus or some stupidity like that? Or maybe their great-grandfather went into the jungle and stole the Holy Ruby out of the Great God Yak's navel, and evil rays are now striking down the kin, one by one?"

She said softly, "What do *you* think is happening?"

"I'll tell you what I think!" he said explosively. "The eldest brother ate too much and jammed up his blood vessels with fatty deposits and got himself an embolism! The sister? An old spinster who got her fill of loneliness!"

"But you wanted to do a book on them because they were ill-fated!" she reminded him. " 'The inside-out story of a strange family.' Those were your very words!"

He suddenly grinned down at her. "I've taken your position, you've taken mine. That's life in a democracy. Let's go get a cup of coffee."

Sam said, "Well! Dave! I'm glad you came over. Would you like some coffee? Coke? Miss Halper's got a regular canteen in the sideroom."

David said, "I went to the synagogue this morning."

"What? Oh! That's fine!" He thought, what's with him now?

David said, "The doors were closed. Locked."

Sam said, "Well, after all! The neighborhood! It's changed! They've got to think of the insurance." He saw the strange smile on his brother's face and he thought, has he been drinking? This early?

David Elias shook his head slowly from side to side. He said, "I stood there and I laughed! I laughed so hard!"

Sam looked nervously toward the door. If Miss Halper walked in – that crazy look in David's eyes – he said quickly, "I've got a pretty heavy morning, Dave – "

"I want you to hear this!" David exclaimed. His bony fingers were scuttling crabs. "I turned to God and the door was locked! It's all part of the one joke, Sam! *Their* joke!"

Sam suddenly remembered something he had read in the paper in Dr. Alvarez's column – "their" was paranoia. He decided to sit down and take it easy and listen, make no fuss, let his young brother say what he pleased, how he pleased, because this was no time to open another door.

"Put it all together!" David Elias demanded. He thrust his face across the desk at his brother. "The whole thing! Suddenly there's the Bomb! Suddenly there's the Hate, black, white, brown, yellow! Suddenly there's the kids and the Drugs – pot, LSD, Speed! Suddenly there's Business back to dog-eat-dog, grabbing and swallowing everything in sight! Suddenly it's everybody, running without faith or hope, running, running to the cliff! Why? Ask yourself – why?"

Sam thought, how can I get him to go see Dr. Finkle? He needs sedatives.

"Think, Sam!" Veins distended, tight skin blood-flushed. "Not for yourself! We're the weeds! She's – she's the flower! Remember – not even Mama ever tried anything with Mary! That means there's hope for *her*! Send her away, Sam! Now! While there's still

time! Don't look at me as if I was crazy! I've thought it out carefully! Mary's the one we've got to save! Do it, Sam!"

Ten minutes later Sam stood by his desk, aspirin bottle in
hand. He couldn't quite remember the dialogue he had used to
get his brother out of the place, but whatever soothing words he
had offered, they had been effective.

Sam thought, it's all been too much for him. I swear I don't
know what he was talking about. I never do. In the old country
he'd have been the scholar of the family, the important one, with
that little cap on his head and a shawl over his shoulders and full
of day-long discussions on how many angels could dance on the
point of a needle. . . . Funny, ever since he left, I'm sweating.
I think I need a drink. Mary should hear that! But I honestly
need a drink. That bottle of Scotch I found in Nat's bottom
drawer. What did I – yeah, here it is. Water? No, I'd better not
make a fuss; drink it straight out of the bottle quick before Miss
Halper . . .

He lifted the bottle to his lips, drank, coughed, wiped his
mouth, and with a hasty look at the door, recapped the bottle
and put it back in the bottom drawer.

He walked to the window and looked out as he thought,
Mary doesn't have to worry. I'll never make a good drunk. Don't
like the taste. . . . Why in the hell am I so upset? What did he
say to me? Nothing new! That business ethics are a pile of bull-
shit? That the atom bomb thing's a nightmare? That kids are
going nuts with crazy sex and pills and pot and the sewer we've
made of their world? So it's always been a crazy world. The
whole idea, a ball spinning around another burning ball – that's
crackpot right to start with!

He sighed deeply and turned to his desk. He thought, I've got
enough troubles without putting the whole world on my back.
Mary – what the hell was he saying about Mary? That she's the
greatest? Don't I know that? So what am I supposed to rescue
her from – tears, tragedy – that's life, always was, always will be.
Listen to me! I'm turning into a two-bit philosopher!

He pressed an intercom button. "Miss Halper, bring your
shorthand book."

After the waitress had taken their order, Tony placed some bills on the table in front of Robin. He said, "The cab fare. I was a jerk, senior grade."

He finally accepted the fact that she would not take the money; as he pocketed the bills, he said, "Let's forget the Elias family for a while. Do you want a really great story for your magazine?"

When she told him she could use one, he went on to ask her if she'd ever been to a Teen-age Fair, the annual extravaganza aimed at the affluent young. "They open tonight at the Palladium on Sunset Boulevard. They'll be setting up exhibits all day. You might want to do a story on the commercial wolves closing in on the teen-agers. Let's go there now."

She was in a mood to be told what to do after that sleepless night; he hailed a cab and made small talk as they headed for the Fair site. She listened and quietly enjoyed his stories about his television experiences; the time he rode the station's traffic-control helicopter and, at five thousand feet, discovered that the pilot had mistaken a sedative for a pep pill and was dozing off; about recording a Mojave Desert gathering of flying-saucer aficionados which had exploded with excitement when an extra-terrestrial disc had flown over them – a vehicle from outer space that had turned out to be a garbage-can lid sailed into the air by a nonbeliever hidden behind a rock.

They reached the Palladium and passed through the gates on the open sesame of Tony's press card; inside Robin found a scene of high activity. The ballroom where, on weekends, Lawrence Welk dispensed waltzes and polkas for middle-aged tourists, was now festooned with psychedelic banners and bunting and posters; the curved walls echoed with a bouillabaisse of ripping saws, workmen's shouts, tapping hammers, and young, bearded, leather-jacketed musicians tuning up through overloaded loud-speakers.

Tony Dumont went off into the melee in the company of old friends from the broadcast booth; Robin wandered away by herself into a world of large and small booths full of glistening Japanese motor bikes, fluorescent-colored paper dresses, racks festooned with arrays of love beads, elaborate exhibits of teen-age makeup, and such a miscellany of revolving lights, beating drums, and pulsing backdrops that soon her eyes and her head were an ache in which, happily, there was room only for the now. It was a world a thousand light-years away from evil and death and loneliness and fear; by the time Tony Dumont caught up with her, she was out in the open area wandering amid the Mile Long Hot Dog booths, the Guess Your Weight and Test Your Strength concessions, and all the other distractions of the open-air entertainment section.

"Hey! You look happy!" Tony greeted her.

She told him that she adored fairs of all sorts; the State Fair, back home, had been a place of wonder to her all through her childhood years.

"Hey! Don't tell me those dainty hands have slopped pigs and won 4-H prizes," he grinned.

She told him no, nothing of that sort; then she confessed that, as a ten-year-old, she had entered the junior jelly-making contest and won a third place ribbon for her choke-cherry.

He grinned down at her. "You know, you're something special. An old-fashioned girl. Put you on display here and who would believe it?"

"I don't believe all this," she told him. "I saw that the sign says two dollars' admission. Do they really pay that, the children?"

"Do they!" he said. "In the three days half a million kids'll come through those turnstiles."

"But why?" she asked. "Everything has a commercial tag on it. There's nothing here, except the rides and the amateur band competition, that they can't see for nothing in the shops along Hollywood Boulevard, or the Strip, or in Sears Roebuck!"

"Don't look for logic," he said. "Commercial? What do they give a damn, as long as it's commercials just for them? In a city that tries to put them down, here they're up. So they pay their two bucks, these ten- to seventeen-year-olds, and they sweat and they yell, and for a little while it's their special world!"

He stopped suddenly and pointed to an ornate tent. "And the ironic thing about it is it's all a variation of the same old pitch! The Establishment must have had those even in Minnesota!"

She saw that the tent was decorated with cabalistic signs and figures; a huge banner screamed:

MADAME CRISTOBLE
YOUR FORTUNE TOLD WHILE YOU WAIT!
LOOK INTO THE FUTURE!
WILL YOU BE RICH? FAMOUS? LOVED?
SEE MADAME CRISTOBLE!

He said, "Hey, Lady Nostradamus herself is in there! Want to go in?"

Robin said quickly, "No, thank you."

He said, "Why not? It's all in fun. She looks in your past and future and tells you exactly what she thinks you want to hear."

Robin said, "No." She shivered. "Could we go now?"

Tony gave her a long look. There was a blast of amplified guitar strings against the beat of multiple drums. "Okay. The Los Angeles Symphony is getting to me."

Detective First Class Mark Moore pulled the sheet from the typewriter, read it, and decided that he was becoming quite a writer in his old age – the Chief would appreciate that touch about "voluntary rape." He settled back in the creaky chair. Life, so far this day, at least, was good. The right kidney was quiescent, and ever since he listened to Anna and bought those expensive – what the hell were they called? – astronaut shoes, his bunions no longer hurt. At the thought of Anna he felt warmth along his loins as his nerve-ends remembered their post midnight love-making when, weary of the television late movie, he had walked into the bathroom to find those voluptuous, uncorseted hips.

He picked up a pen, and as he signed the report, he wondered, as always, what his fellow officers would say if they found out that the name on his birth certificate was actually Marco De La More, a well-kept secret known only to him and an ancient file in the Chief's office.

The telephone at his elbow jingled. At the voice in the phone he straightened up. He said briskly, "Yes, sir. . . . Yes, sir. I've already checked into it. Copy of autopsy report is right here on my desk. Suicide straight and simple . . . Yes, sir, I agree with you. But there's nothing to warrant further investigation. Just a family of losers, that's all."

★

As soon as they were on their way in a cab, Tony turned to her and said, "I want to ask you a direct question. I hope you give me a direct answer. What's bothering you? Or, to put it in the language of the natives, what's bugging you?"

Robin said, "Nothing. Nothing at all."

He said, "Of course I expected that answer. So I'll ask you an even more direct question. Who is he?" At her look: "The one who makes your smile a very rare thing."

She looked at him and her eyes blurred and he wasn't there, and she was back home and the telephone was ringing. As it had rung that day. The moment she had heard his mother's broken voice she had known. "Robin! Robin! . . ."

The world had dissolved into tears; then the heart-tearing walk by the lake shore where she and Howard had parted; hours later she had gone home, packed, and taken the first plane westward. Somewhere she had read that in Southern California was to be found the largest aggregation of spiritualists, mystics, clairvoyants, and all the others who sought to look behind the dark curtain.

She arrived in Los Angeles on a Sunday; she took an airport bus to the Hollywood hotel the driver suggested; the window of her room framed tourists examining movie-star footprints in the forecourt of the stucco-pillared movie palace across the street.

She had bought a Sunday paper at the airport; now she covered the bed with a print-smudged snowdrift of newsprint before she found what she sought – the pages filled with religious news and advertisements of services.

A half hour later a cab had left her off at the First Church of Religious Spiritualism. The metered fare had been shockingly high, and the status of the neighborhood, it was apparent, frighteningly low. The buildings, including the blackened limestone one to which she had been brought, huddled together in the misery of mutual decay.

Robin climbed a short flight of worn stone steps and shivered in a swirl of dirt-laden wind. Beyond a door was another door with a worn plaque stating "Church Entrance"; through the second door she found herself in a dark pit; on a small stage a skeletal man in a white suit was exhorting the audience to believe.

Robin stood self-consciously in the rear until her eyes accommodated enough to see aisles; she moved into one of them, stumbled over legs, begged pardons, sat in a lap, jumped up, and, finally, gratefully, found a hard seat beneath her.

The cadaverous man on the stage echoed, "And now, sistern and brethren, before Sister Maybelle communicates with your loved ones, we will give generously to the Lord and ask that He free the blessed spirits to come among us."

A hidden electronic organ began a heavy-handed dirge; someone jostled Robin's elbow and she saw a tray in front of her. She took it, fumbled in her purse, dropped a bill into the container, then passed it on into the gloom at her right.

The dim light onstage suddenly went into deeper gloom; Robin sat very still as a very large woman, swathed in black, glided on-stage, her long skirt shielding her feet so that she seemed to be moving on invisible wheels. She came up to a straight-backed chair stage center as the white-suited man dragged a table in front of her; when the woman seated herself, warped boards groaned at the concentrated weight.

Robin looked quickly, nervously about her; she saw that there were no more than fifteen or twenty in the audience; apparently she had stumbled into the one row that had more than a sprinkling of people.

She took another glance about; the morning sun struggled to enter windows encrusted with the city's fallout. She saw that there was grime everywhere, dirt and dust all about her, and she thought, oh, my darling, why would you come to me here and not in the bright, fresh cleanness of our lake?

The fat woman on the stage was sitting rigidly, head bowed. The white-suited man's voice lowered two octaves; he said, "I beg of you complete silence. The spirits are waiting."

Suddenly the seated woman began to moan eerily; Robin tensed as the thin sound echoed at her side. In the dimness she saw that a very aged woman, seated to the left beyond one empty seat, was moaning to herself almost in unison with the medium on the stage.

"I am here!" The words burst from the medium's throat in a bass roar that lifted Robin off the seat.

"Nakowa is here!" the voice continued. "Me wantum speak initials R.J.!"

The old woman to Robin's left squealed. She cried out in a cracked voice, "Here! My darling, I am here!"

The loud voice on the stage went on: "Do not worry. I am very happy. Very happy."

"Praise the Lord!" wept the old woman.

The white suit loomed behind the medium. "There are so many messages from beyond this morning that we must ask that R.J. remain after the services for a special private séance."

"Oh, I will, I will!" the old woman cried.

Robin gasped as something caressed her thigh. She looked sharply to her right. The seat had been empty; a man with a face like fat bacon was there. She jumped to her feet. She stumbled past the sobbing old woman down the aisle as behind her on the stage an old voice was calling out, "If you are a Sensitive, stay! Stay!"

The following day she telephoned the number the City Editor of the Minneapolis paper had given her and, by the end of the week, through his influence, she was, wonder of wonders, a file clerk in the beehive of *The Los Angeles Times*.

She did not want to repeat the error of her first contact with spiritualism; she avidly began to read every book she could find on the subject of spirits and spiritualism.

She obtained a library card and took out as many books as possible, broadening the base of her interest to include psychical research, mysticism, the Oriental occult, and related subjects.

Early in her reading she discovered that spiritualism, and research into survival after death, went far beyond that dirty, dusty little hall and its white-suited barker, its fat woman, and its pale little man with wandering hands.

Great names had believed in survival after death. Not just men of religion, but also scientists, authors, statesmen – Sir Oliver Lodge and Elizabeth Barrett Browning and the renowned physicist Sir William Crookes, and hundreds of others.

The more she read on the subject, the more puzzled Robin became. It was true. It wasn't true. Ghosts (How can you be that, Howard?) were lonely figures walking in ancient English gardens. Ghosts were hallucinations triggered by wish-thinking. (Yes, I wish, Howard, I wish!) Ghosts were souls unable to rest in Paradise until they communicated a last request. (I'm waiting, Howard!) Ghosts were illusions brought on by emotional distress, fatigue, or unconscious self-hypnosis. (Call it anything, if I could only see you once more, my darling!)

After many weeks she decided to conduct her own séance; she sat for hours in her darkened room, nerve-ends straining, waiting for a whisper, a touch. Night after night, each session ending in bitter tears of frustration and loneliness.

She began to read the spiritualism advertisements once again, their carefully worded suggestions of miracles to be performed. But she went to none of the billboarded meetings; she had an instinct that if a charlatan tricked her with even a far-fetched approximation of Howard's voice or words, her small trust fund security would quickly evaporate in a whirlwind of expensive private séances.

She began to wonder if there was a psychical society where she could inquire for a legitimate medium, but a search of the telephone listings indicated no such group, and she was too self-conscious to expose herself to the cynicism of the reporters at the newspaper.

So she gradually and regretfully put away the thought of communicating with her fiancé's spirit, but sometimes, in the melancholia of night, she would dream of a transparent Howard, walking through great basalt mountains, trying to reach her.

Tony Dumont's voice from somewhere in space: "Hi! Robin! I've asked you a question, remember?"

His face, the cab, the passing scene, slipped into focus; she said, "I – I'm sorry."

He said, "Okay, delete my question. It's none of my long-nosed business, anyway."

It had been pent up too long. She said, "I want to tell you."

If he had reacted in any other manner than the way he did – a silent, neutral look – she would not have gone on; now she began to speak, quickly, compulsively, of Howard, of the voice at the lake, her coming to Hollywood, her search for a bridge from this world to her love.

When the guileless flow of words had ended, Tony Dumont remained silent. The taxi pulled up before the apartment house; he paid the driver, then helped Robin out.

He said, "There's so much to say. May I come up?"

She looked at his solemn face. She nodded.

They started up the stairs together.

Chapter 10

Mary thought, he's gotten as thin as a letter opener. No, he looks like a holy man.

"How nice of you to come over," she told him.

"Why are you still here?" he demanded.

She thought, and where was I supposed to go? And why is he speaking in a whisper?

"Are you getting a cold?" she asked him.

He shook his head.

She said, "I'll get you some coffee. Or maybe you'd like some tea?"

David Elias looked around. "The children?" he asked.

Mary said, "As usual. In Mark's room. Won't you sit down?"

She suddenly realized that he was extremely agitated; he sat on the edge of the couch swaying back and forth as if in inner prayer.

She smiled reassuringly as she said, "You haven't answered me. Which will it be? Coffee, tea, or milk? I sound like an airline stewardess!"

He said, "Why didn't you listen to Sam?"

Mary said, "And what was he supposed to tell me?"

He was on his feet again, his hands waving excitedly as he spoke. "I should have realized! He wouldn't! Maybe there's still time! Go! Go!"

Mary Elias said, "Dave, please! You're shouting!" She thought, he must have been drinking! But he was so close to her that she could smell his breath, and there was no alcohol on it. But his eyes were bright, feverish, and his face was heavily flushed.

She said, "Please, Dave. Please sit down. Whatever you want to tell me, I'll listen, but please sit down. There's plenty of time."

He said explosively, "No! I'm telling you! There is no more time! Nat, Harriet, next it'll be me, then Sam! Everything in order, always in order!"

The import of what he had said to her sank through. She said unbelievingly, "You? Sam?"

He said explosively, "Yes! Yes! You're not of her blood! You've got a chance! If you go! Now!"

Mary Elias turned away. "I'll get some coffee."

With a quick step he was up to her, swinging her around. "No! You've got to listen to me! I've got to get through to you! We're finished, all right! But not you! I don't want you to die!"

Mary thought, I wish Sam was here. Aloud she said, with deliberate calmness, "And I don't intend to die. Until my time."

"Then go!" he shouted.

Anger flooded Mary Elias's cheeks, but she kept her voice quiet. "If I understand you correctly, you're telling me to run away. Where? Why?"

"Mama!" he screamed at her, and the word echoed thinly from window to window.

Mary Elias picked the last of the word out of the air. "Mama," she repeated. "The word is a sickness in you, isn't it?" When he tried to speak, she interrupted sharply, "No! You listen to me, David Elias! For years I've stood around and listened while you and your family used Mama to excuse every fault, every weakness in yourselves! Well, no more! You're sick! All right! I understand! It would take someone made out of steel to endure these two weeks without being affected! But enough of your mama and blaming your mama! She's dead, long dead, and whatever happens to you will be of your doing, not hers!"

He looked at her in wonder, almost unbelievingly, and then he stumbled past her, and in spite of her quick protestations, he was gone, the unlatched door swinging back and forth almost in rhythm to the rise and fall of the heterodyne note singing down the hall from the boy's room.

I won't tell Sam, Mary thought as she slowly closed the door. He's endured enough.

He was sitting on the chair where she had found him the morning after Bob Farrell. He had been there, interspersed with rising, and agitated walking up and down, and reseating himself, for an explosive hour, and Robin was wondering how, even for a moment, she had been under the stupid delusion that she could communicate with this man.

She cried out, "Don't look at me as if I were a pinhead! What about that Bishop who talked to his dead son!"

He growled, "What about it?"

She said, "A man of that standing! He's positive he talked to his child!"

He looked at her sadly. "I saw a rerun of the television tape of that séance. Did you?"

"What if I didn't see it?" she demanded. "I read all about it in the newspapers, the news magazines. They quoted him directly!"

"His only son a suicide, a bereaved father believes what he wants to believe." At her grim look: "All right, then why didn't the spirit come directly back to the father? Why did the son have to speak through the mouth of a stranger?"

For a split second the echo of her own thoughts stilled her, then she said, "Because – because some people are sensitives!"

"Yeah, yeah!" he scoffed. "Just the way some people are sensitive to the microwaves of television programs going through them. Look in their eyes and you'll see *Gunsmoke*."

She said, "In the Branfield house, up the road from where I was born, for an entire week things were thrown about! Dishes against the wall and no one there to throw them! Rocks through the air and no one throwing them! I saw it with my own eyes!"

He said, "Oh, sure! The old poltergeist bit. And I'll bet you twenty to one there was a kid in the family who wasn't getting enough attention from Papa or Mama!"

She suddenly remembered owl-faced little Johnny Branfield; she closed her eyes wearily. She said, "There's got to be more than just *this*."

He said, "Because you want it that way?"

She thought, I will not cry, not in front of this unfeeling man.

He spoke again, so softly that she leaned toward him as she listened.

He said, "All right. That was cruel." He looked beyond her. "It even happened once to Tony the Skeptic. I lay there in the night waiting for her whisper." He got to his feet. He walked to the window. His back was rigid. He said grimly, "I was slightly insane. There are no multiple planes of existence. Just this. To think anything else is to degrade reason."

Robin said, "But you don't *know!*"

He looked back at her. He said, "You're very sweet. And naïve. And lucky. That you didn't get into the hands of one of the thousands of crystal-gazing, ectoplasm-waving phonies that infest this town. You were right about one thing. Southern California attracts them all right. The way a manure pile attracts flies. I once wanted to do a whole series exposing the miserable lot. But I got gunned down by management. Why? Because most of the spirit business impresarios operate on a phony religioso basis. Why not? It's their legal armor. They can buy a nice, fresh minister diploma for as little as ten dollars on the line. That's a fact! There's one outfit calls itself The Ministry of Cosmic Wisdom. Ten dollars and you're ordained, licensed to perform all services from marriage, to preaching on any subject you're ignorant about, to materializing Uncle Eddie. And, above all, to passing the collection plate. And if anyone tries to expose you, he's interfering with your constitutional guarantee of freedom of worship!" He turned away from the window. "Fog's coming in. Could I have a cup of coffee? Or point me in the direction of the pot and I'll pour it myself."

Robin blinked, said she was sorry, and headed for the kitchen.

David Elias took a deep breath of the fog-laden air. The sea, to the west, was in it; when he turned the key and entered the house he knew that all that freshness would be gone and the special odor of the familiar rooms would be there.

His legs began to tremble, but he inserted the serrated metal into the cylinder lock and turned it. When he tried the door, it opened swiftly, cleanly, as if eager to envelop him after these many weeks.

He banged the door behind him compulsively as she had always made him do, and he stood there in the gloom, and the smell was there that went beyond the mustiness of old wood and old furnishings, the pungent essence, that had always permeated the very walls, of the things she used to burn.

He stood in the gloom listening. He said softly, tentatively. "Mama?"

Then the word ripped out of him in a great searing shout that tore through the whole house. "*M-a-m-a?*"

He began to run through the house, shrieking the question over and over, stumbling and falling, rising to run again, through room after room, his scrabbling feet raising weary dust. "Mama? Mama?"

Up the canyon of stairs, pounding through the old familiarities of bedrooms and storerooms and secret places. "Mama? Mama?"

Down the stairs again, and now he stood in the dreariness of the front parlor, his chest heaving, his mouth gasping the fetid air.

"You're here, Mama! I know you're here!" His voice began to rise again. "Mama! Answer me, Mama! *Mama!*" He began to run around the house once more, through the rooms, up the stairs and down again, shrieking her name, and soon his voice was a croak and his movements were disjointed, until, at last, he fell in complete exhaustion. But as he lay on the filth of the floor, his legs still moved, and he wept, "Mama! Mama! Let us go! Please let us go, Mama!"

When the coffee was poured and drunk, she said, "In the books I've read, many famous men – statesmen, authors, scientists – have stated their belief in the possibility of the return of the dead."

Tony put the cup down on the end table and stretched his long legs. "Yeah. Famous men. Sir Oliver Lodge among them. They always use him for Exhibit A. But all his life the spirit cons suckered him – including the most famous faker of all, Palladino.

Oh, Sir Oliver wasn't the only one Señora Palladino took down the garden path – she had the great ones all over Europe beating the drum for her direct line to the heavenly pastures. Unfortunately for her, the lady came to America, where a couple of college kids crawled under the table with a hidden flashlight and saw her rapping out those authentic ghostly messages with knee and knuckles. So when word got back to England about the exposure, whom did dear old Sir Oliver believe? The debunkers or the faker? The faker, of course. Because Sir Oliver was an old man – he *wanted* to believe. There's the key to it all, Robin. People want so desperately to believe in existence after death that they sit in those darkened room séances with every nerve-end begging for substantiation of what they want to see and hear. Expose the medium, show them that any competent magician can duplicate the ghost photos, the sealed-slate chalk writings, the knockings and the trumpet calls, and they'll still believe. They'll find a million rationalizations to explain away the exposé – and head for the next spiritualist who promises them a contact with their beloved departed. I bleed when I say this, Robin, but it's a multimillion racket pure and simple. I'd give my tarnished soul to be able to tell you – and myself – differently. But the dead are dead, and they'll rest in death until time itself is gone!"

Her head was lowered; he suddenly realized that she was crying silently. He came closer to her. He said agonizedly, "I can't help it! I can't lie! To you – or myself! I've watched the fakers at work. I've listened to them talk among themselves when the lights were on. They count up the take and have a glass of beer and laugh at the fools they've just conned!"

Robin lifted an unhappy face. She said, "If all the world were deaf and there were one singer, would you deny the existence of the song?"

Tony sighed. "That's an ancient argument. But we're not talking about living beings. We're discussing disembodied spirits."

"They have to reach us through human beings!"

Tony said softly, "I'll ask it again. I'm somewhat human. Why should my lost love go among strangers?"

Robin looked up at him. Her eyes were strangely searching.

He said quickly, "What is it?"

She said, "The girl. You loved. Was her name . . ." She hesitated a split second, then she asked, "Eileen?"

After a long breath he said softly, "How did you know that?"

Robin said, "I – I don't know."

Tony Dumont said emphatically, "There's a case in point! For a moment you had me going! But the explanation's a simple one! Somewhere along the line, since I've met you, I've said the name, and you heard it, and your subconscious filed it away."

She said, "*Did* you say it?"

"Not consciously, perhaps, but in thinking of her, I may have mouthed the word without realizing it. The way some people read. You've seen them. Their lips form the words, and they don't know they're doing it. Your eyes read my lips and remembered. Or you may have actually heard me unconsciously whisper the name. That's the very phenomenon that has discredited so many of those extra-sensory tests. The pick-a-card routine. Objective investigators have found that some of the best subjects – the ones who get phenomenal scores in supposed thought transference or clairvoyance – have extraordinary hearing. They don't realize it, but they actually hear the other person sitting behind a screen or in another room unconsciously saying what the card or the object might be. That may have happened between you and me! You heard – you remembered!"

Robin was suddenly very weary. She closed her eyes.

Tony said, "You must be very tired. Forgive me. One thing more and I'll go. When I got here this morning and told you that Harriet Elias was dead, I thought I heard you say, 'I know.' I came here the moment the flash came over the teletype. How did you know about it before I got here?"

Robin found the energy with which to speak. "The children told me. The Elias children. I was there yesterday."

Tony said slowly, "Yesterday? When yesterday?"

She said, "It was late. In the afternoon."

Tony said, "Are you sure?"

She said tiredly, "Yes. The grown-ups were at the funeral. Only the children were home."

Tony exclaimed, "But Harriet Elias died last night! Don't look at me like that! It's a fact! *Last night!* How could the children possibly have told you that she had died the night before?"

Robin said carefully, "I may have mistaken what they said."

He shrugged. "Of course! Well, it's been a long afternoon. I hope not too unhappy a one for you." He looked down at her. "Confession time. When I said I wanted to collaborate on that novel with you, I really didn't give a damn about the novel. I just wanted to be near you." He turned away.

"Tony," she called softly.

He turned quickly.

She said, "Do you know where she lived? The grandmother?"

He looked his surprise. He said, "Yes. I think I do. Yes. It's in Santa Monica near the ocean. An old house. All the Eliases moved out after she died. Why do you ask?"

"Would you tell me how to get there?"

"Why?"

She looked up at him silently, and he said, "No reason necessary." He reached in his pocket. "I'll draw you a map. When do you intend to go there?"

She said quietly, "I'm not sure."

Sam looked up from his newspaper. "So what's with the Quiet Two?"

Mary said, "They're watching television. I looked in a few minutes ago."

"Did they get outside today?"

Mary said, "I took Shirley shopping with me. We were out about two hours. Then it turned foggy."

"Mark?"

Mary Elias rubbed her forehead. She thought, I don't like this day. First David – now *he* comes home early with questions. She said, "After you left this morning, I told him I wanted him to go outside to get some fresh air. He walked out on the balcony and took six deep breaths and came back in again."

She saw the quick corrugations on his forehead and she added quickly, "If you want him to be an athlete, stay home and do it yourself! I – I can't cope with him!"

Sam threw the paper down on the floor and got to his feet. "Who's talking about being an athlete? Exercise! Any kind of exercise! By the time he's fifteen, he'll have a potbelly and high blood pressure!"

Mary told him not to talk nonsense; when he moved purposefully toward the door, she went after him, saying, "What are you going to do?"

He said, "I'm home, I'll cope with him!"

She stayed a few steps behind him as he went down the hallway toward the children's room. She thought, he's getting too big around the shoulders. I mustn't let him get fat. I couldn't live without him.

As he opened Mark's bedroom door, around Sam's bulk Mary could see the two heads intent on the small screen of the portable. The word "Volcano" appeared on the glass, and a great explosion rattled the loudspeaker.

Sam turned to his wife. "What's this? Some more violence?"

Mary said quickly, "No, no, I read about it in the paper. An educational program. The birth of a volcano somewhere."

"They don't even know we're in the room," Sam muttered.

A stentorian voice intoned, over a picture of a placid sea, "In the year 1963, in the quiet sea off Iceland, human eyes saw one of the greatest happenings in all recorded history – the birth of a volcano."

Suddenly, out of the pictured water, a great geyser of molten lava flung itself into the sky as another explosion reverberated.

Mary put her hand on Sam's arm. She whispered, "Talk to him after the program. He was telling Shirley about this at breakfast."

Sam muttered, "Okay, okay! As soon as it's over, you tell him what's what!" He turned and stalked out of the room.

Mary thought, I'm elected again. Mary the discipline-giver.

She said, "All right, children! As soon as this program is over, out you go! That's an order!"

The small heads did not turn; Mary said, "I really mean it! Outside! There's hours of daylight left and – and I promised your father!"

Again they ignored her; Mary Elias felt sudden, unaccustomed fury. How dare they! She had been much too permissive, particularly the last few weeks. All right, this was the end of that!

She moved toward the television set. She would turn it off. At once!

On the screen a great whirlpool had formed in the boiling sea; out of it crawled a viscous stream of molten magma, twisting and turning like a beast out of a nightmare.

As Mary Elias came up to the set, small bodies crashed past her and knelt in front of the screen.

"Beautiful! Oh, it's beautiful!" Mark cried out.

"Beautiful!" echoed Shirley.

"And it's red! I know it's red! Beautiful red!" Mark exulted.

Mary Elias reached down, seized her son by his arms, and pulled him to his feet. "Stop that! Stop that now!" she cried out through his continuing babble.

His face was turned toward the lava, and when she said, "Look at me!" and cupped his chin and pulled him around toward her, she saw, in horror, that his eyes were red-flecked, and she let go of him. She looked at the screen, but it was no reflection – the picture was still black-and-white.

She cried out, "Sam! Sam!" and in answer to the high note of fear, he was there in seconds demanding to know what was the matter.

She could not speak, but through the roaring in her head she heard Mark's calm voice saying, "The program frightened her. I've turned it off."

And when she opened her eyes and looked at her son, Mary saw that his eyes were as cerulean blue as they ever had been.

Chapter 11

Long tentacles of fog had moved in from the ocean, met, coalesced, and thickened.

Although it was early in the afternoon, Robin found herself turning on the lights of her car. By the time she was within a mile of the address Tony had given her, she was isolated in a blur of white stretching endlessly before her, the auto's headlights reflecting back futilely from the drifting curtain.

Her straining eyes finally glimpsed a corner lamp post and

she stopped her car next to it. She left the lights on full, with the motor running, and got out. She could see the street sign only by standing up close to the water-dripping iron post; she saw that she was on a street close to the number Tony had written.

In the few moments that had elapsed, the fog had thickened, and when she turned back to her car, she could barely see its outline. She reached in, turned off the engine, then locked the doors from the outside. The ache behind her eyes was evidence enough of the strain of this blind piloting; she would walk to her destination.

As she began to move along the sidewalk, she saw that the fog was hanging a few inches above the cement; when another pedestrian suddenly passed her, she saw disembodied feet moving to her, then away.

She strained her eyes for house signs, but it was hopeless. She would have to find the path to each house in turn and go up to the very door in order to read numbers. She decided that she was in the middle of the block; she began to look downward for a path that would indicate a house. She suddenly bumped into something huge; she cried out as rough cloth and arms enveloped her; then she heard Tony Dumont's voice. "Don't be frightened. It's Tony Dumont."

Gratefully she saw his face through the mist. He said, "I had a hunch you'd do it right away. Don't be angry."

She said, "Oh, no, I'm not angry. Please, where is the house?"

His large hand was reassuringly under her elbow; the fog clawed at them as he piloted her down a crunching gravel path. Robin could see nothing of the building until they were actually on the porch; from there she saw weatherbeaten wood siding on either side of an ancient door.

Tony said, "You know, of course, this place has been un-occupied for months."

As he said it, his hand went to the door. He added lightly, "If the door isn't locked and the hinges creak, I'll scream."

He turned the knob, and the heavy wood moved aside quite noiselessly.

Tony did a Jack Benny, "Well!" Then he said, "Want to go in?"

Robin breathed, "Yes." Tony opened the door fully and they

went through. The hallway was dimly lit from a skylight high above. Tony said, "Is this the proper time to ask you why you wanted to come here?"

Robin looked at the gloom of the place; a staircase crawled darkly upward and a gloomy entry gaped to the left. She had no real answer; she said, "I'm not sure."

Then she gasped and she felt Tony's grip tighten on her arm. Someone was descending the steps. In the dark it was hard to see details; a vague, grayish figure, closer and closer.

Then she saw who it was. She said happily, "It's Mr. Elias! I'm Robin Shepherd, Mr. Elias." The man slowly advanced toward them. "You remember, I interviewed your nephew. And Mr. Dumont. He was there, too."

David Elias said tonelessly, "Please shut the door."

Robin heard Tony close the door behind her; she said with forced brightness, "I hope we're not intruding. We wanted to see your old home."

Tony came back alongside her. Dave Elias said, "Please come in," again in that empty voice, and Robin wondered if he was ill.

He led the way into the gloom of what was obviously the parlor. The floor was littered and the walls were of a dismal dark overlay of discolored cloth.

Dave Elias said, "Please sit down."

He said it not as a host greeting a guest, but in so lifeless a voice that once again Robin wondered whether the man was not well.

She sat down on the wooden box he had indicated; Tony Dumont came up and stood by her as Dave Elias moved to the smoke-stained fireplace.

Somewhere, deep in the house, something fell; after that there was no sound. Robin looked upward and saw that the only light in the room was filtering through high, partly shuttered leaded windows. She thought, why am I no longer afraid? I didn't want to come here. But I had to. There's nothing. An old empty house – and I'm not as frightened here as I was in their bright new apartment.

Dave Elias suddenly spoke. He said, "I don't mind your coming here. It makes no difference."

Tony Dumont said, "Then I'm sure you won't mind my asking you a few questions."

Robin looked at him in amazement. What was this?

David Elias's white face turned slowly to the other man.

"Was the murder committed here in this house?" Tony asked.

Robin wanted to cry out, "But the woman was acquitted!" but even as she reacted in thought, David Elias said, "Yes."

Robin looked up at Tony; she saw that he was as amazed as she was by the flat, unexpected statement.

"I saw it happen," David Elias said.

Tony Dumont found his voice. "But you didn't tell the police!"

The sad eyes moved back to him. "How do you tell the police that your mother has committed a murder?"

"Was your brother's death a murder? And your sister's?" Tony demanded.

David Elias said slowly, "No. Not in the sense you would think of murder."

"Then in what sense were they murdered?" Tony persisted.

David Elias suddenly cupped his hands over his face. He stood, head bowed, his body shaking convulsively.

In all of her life Robin had never seen a grown man cry; the sight and the sound of this one weeping so passionately was suddenly unbearable. She wanted to get up and run from the place, shut it all away with the closing of that weather-beaten outer door.

Dave Elias lifted his face from his hands. He said, with difficulty, "I want you to understand. I do not weep for myself."

Tony Dumont had been standing, watching intently. Now he said flatly, "Tell us."

Dave Elias said, "Why should I endanger you?"

Robin thought swiftly – endanger? There was no danger in this old place. She felt nothing here, nothing but gloom and neglect and decay.

Tony Dumont repeated, "Tell us."

The older man moved back to the mantelpiece and took a book from the ledge. He took two steps forward and held it out. "Do you know what book this is?" He brought it a step closer.

Tony said, "It looks like some sort of Bible."

Dave Elias said, "God's book. I brought it here before I knew." He opened his fingers, and Robin gasped as the volume thudded on the floor. "There are those who say God is dead." He shook his head. "He is not dead. He is blind." His pinched face turned toward Robin. "His eyes were burned out by the fires in the concentration camps, by the hell over Hiroshima. And when he found out that he was blind, do you know what God did? He turned His back on the world and He stumbled into space and He ran and He ran and He is still running far, far out at the edges of nowhere. Lost to us forever!"

Robin thought, Tony, why is he saying these terrible things to us? What does he mean by them? God is here! He is with us! Always!

"And in that moment God left the earth, what else do you think happened?" The small man's voice became a searing rasp. "*They* came out of hiding! The devils! All the demons who had been living behind masks since the beginning of time! The world was theirs, suddenly theirs! Since the day when the mountains were fire, whenever He had a spare moment, God had been hunting them out, tearing them out from their hiding places, driving them one by one into the chasms of Hell. But now He is gone! And the devils are free on earth! Free in high and low places to do as they will without fear of God's great retribution!" He stopped suddenly and looked at each of them in turn. "You don't think I know what I'm talking about, do you? Don't you understand? I am an authority on devils! My mama was one of them!"

Robin thought, no, no more! Tony, please! Let us go!

The rasping voice went inexorably on. "She was born in evil, my mama, and she lived in evil, and when she decided to go, she departed in evil! And God is not here anymore to help us with the terrible legacy she left us!"

Tony Dumont exploded. "What the hell are you talking about? Evil? What is evil? It's only an abstraction, a word, a label!"

Dave Elias said sadly, "You cannot understand . . ."

Tony Dumont said, "Oh, yes, I do! It's a word with less stability than any other in our language! What's an abomination in one breath of history becomes permissible in the next!" Robin saw him take a deep, stabilizing breath before he went on. "Mr.

Elias, you've had a great deal to endure. *But there are no devils!* Your mother may have been many things, but a devil? No! Just a sick human being! Accept that fact! Then forget it and go live your own life!"

Dave Elias said slowly, almost in pity, "The scientific. The rational."

Tony Dumont said, "And you need a big dose of it! All right, you talk glibly of devils! Let's talk some more about them! What are they? Your own fears, nothing more! Man's done that all through history – every time he feared something, he created a new demon to take the blame. Thunder, lightning, eclipses, floods, earthquakes, plagues – everything he couldn't explain became a demon's work! And when he began to understand natural forces, he took the blame away from the devils – yes, and he replaced the thunder and lightning and all the rest with the moral issues – he hung the monkeys of lust and lechery, madness and every other variety of human frailty and sickness on a devil's back!"

Robin thought, Tony, don't argue with him about devils! Please! Tell him of God, a great God, a just God, all-seeing, forgiving and giving!

"The devil is the mainstay of religion," Tony went on. "Every faith has had to invent the devil myth all over again or steal it from the garbage heap of the civilization they overcame or destroyed. From the Valley of the Nile, to India, to China, and back to the Nordics – every religious group built a Hell and filled it with devils to keep their believers in line! Christianity took the Devil from the Jews and made him an even greater monster and gave him an even deeper Hell – but it's the same old fantasy that you're using today in your own fear and your own pain!" His arms encompassed the gloom. "Why do you come to this place? Sell it! Give it away! Go where there's sun and reality! Go now!"

Dave Elias said vaguely, "Yes. My brother Sam is waiting for me."

Tony said, "Would you like us to take you to him?"

The older man looked at him and at Robin who had risen to her feet. He said, "No." Then he added, "Did you hear? My nephew can bring back the voices of the dead." He turned away.

In a few seconds they heard the sound of the outer door. Tony said, "Let's get out of here. A family of kooks!"

He went on talking as he led her through the entry-room to the door, but Robin was no longer listening to him. There was something in the air, just beyond hearing. Then it was there, distant but distinct. A cat. The mew of a cat.

She started to tell Tony about it, but by then he had closed the door behind them and the sound was gone. She saw that approaching night had darkened the fog; she and the man next to her were suspended in gray space.

She heard Tony say, "What's wrong? Didn't you hear me?"

She said, "I'm sorry. What did you say?"

He said, "I said that when we find your car, let's go somewhere where there's light and music and good food and drinks."

She said, not looking at him, "No. Thank you."

He asked, "Why not? Haven't you had enough of gloom and my stupid lectures for a day?"

She said, "I want to go back to the children."

He said unbelievingly, "The Elias children?"

"Please."

"But why?"

"If Mr. Elias has been saying those terrible things to them, I want to talk to them of God."

Tony Dumont took a deep breath. He said, "It's been that kind of day. Okay!"

"Sam."

"Huh?"

"Two bathrooms and you still wash in the kitchen?"

"I keep telling you – it's one of those whachamacallits? – conditioned reflexes." He looked at her. "That's not why you said, 'Sam.'"

"You're too smart."

"Okay, let's have it."

She took a deep breath. "Their eyes are shining."

"Wha-at?"

"Their eyes. It's as if they had a . . . a fever. But I took their temperatures and they're perfectly normal."

Sam grinned. "You know, the older you get, the more you talk a kind of shorthand."

"Sam, I'm serious!"

"I don't know what you're talking about! You took their temperatures and they're perfectly normal! Their eyes were shining! So okay, it's spring! And they went outside for a coupla hours and had some exercise for a change! Hey, what is this? Potato salad?"

"Keep your hands off. It's for tonight. David's coming over."

"What do you mean – tonight? I'm hungry now."

"All right, but take a spoon. And not too much. You're fat enough."

As Sam, grumbling that he was not fat, just muscular, went after a plate and a fork, Mary thought, oh, Sam, how can I explain it to you? Words again! Ever since the volcano thing. The way they've looked. That eager, waiting look. The way we used to look when we were kids on Christmas Eve. But now it's spring. And when I asked him, he just shrugged and looked at me with those eyes. And when I asked Shirley, all she did was giggle. But it wasn't her usual kind of giggle. If I told Sam that, he'd say, "Now that's really silly! How many kinds of giggle can a little girl have?" And I haven't any answer. Except one. Does it have something to do with *her*? Now *I'm* doing it! Talking the way *they* do! Making her the scapegoat for everything! She was never anything but nice to me. Never! But I'm frightened! Of what? A giggle? A look?

She said, "Sam!"

"Huh?"

"Could we go away?"

He repeated, "Away?"

"Yes. A little vacation. Anywhere."

He came close to her and put his hands on her shoulders. "Yeah. Okay. Saturday."

She thought, Saturday. Can I endure it until Saturday? Endure what? My daughter? My son?

"Hey, Mary, what's the matter? Why are you closing your eyes all of a sudden?"

She opened them quickly. She said, "Because they're tired.

Watching you stuff yourself. Get out of the kitchen, please. I've got work to do."

As he steered the car through the thinning fog, Tony Dumont said derisively, "Me, expert on evil and the devil! I did it quote for quote straight out of a radio show I did about a year ago! You'd be surprised how many subjects I can sound off on without real knowledge – for a maximum of fifteen minutes less commercials!" He snorted. "Did you hear what he said? 'Voices of the dead.' That would be pretty fascinating. The record companies would come out with cassettes of the one and only true version of 'The Sermon on the Mount' in stereo. Simulated stereo, of course."

Robin thought about that untruth about God, blinded, groping in infinite space. . . .

As if he were listening to her thought, Tony suddenly said, "And that bit about God leaving the earth. I wanted to ask him, 'When was He ever here?'"

Robin said, "Don't you believe in God?"

He blinked. He kept his eyes on the glistening road. He said, "How is that pertinent to this conversation?"

She said, "I just want to know."

He said, "I believe in miracles. The miracle of people. Four billion years ago molecules of gas made love in space – and here we are."

"And God?" she asked.

He smiled. "You *are* an innocent. Your counterpart walked through the filth of the ages and saw only a great shining glory above." He let out a deep breath. "Heaven help you!" He gave her a quick glance. "Or maybe I should."

"And is God in that heaven?"

"A very innocent, *persistent* person," he amended. "Okay. Answers. First a question? Why must I believe? I once went to a Holy Follow Me meeting where the Leader-man told the audience he could turn water into wine. He poured the water into a glass, then he cried out, 'Faithful, do you believe your Leader can turn water into wine?'

"'Yeah, verily we do!' the Faithful answered.

" 'Then if you believe, I don't have to do it,' yelled the preacher – and passed the collection plate.

"Okay, I'll admit I believe. In reason. Ultimate reason. On earth if we don't fission it. Then why do I have to discuss heaven?"

"Reason is not enough. You must have faith in the Almighty!"

"Which Almighty?" he asked her. "My, my, I haven't had to talk like this since the bull sessions at school when I was very young. The God of fire and fury and vengeance of the Hebrews? The militant God of Christianity who watches over the fall of sparrows and shrugs at the slaughter, in less than two thousand years, of fifty million human beings? David Elias said God was not dead, just blinded. He's wrong. God has died in our time. As other Gods have died in other times. Dead Osiros, and dead Tammuz, dead Manitou, dead Ishtar, and dead Moloch, and dead Odin – dead, dead! – deified for a small breath of history, and now dead, the way all Gods must die. Don't you see, each God lives only in the fears of imperfect men, and when those fears die in the bodies of those men, the God dies with them."

She said, "I pity you."

"Come now!"

"You live in a world without hope."

"Of what?" he wanted to know.

"Of salvation. Of continuity of the human spirit."

He gave her a long look. He said, "I'll take those in reverse. Continuity of the human spirit? The only continuity I believe in is the sperm entering the ovum and the egg cell multiplying until it begets its own eggs or sperm and continues the process. The fact of the matter is, I don't even quite believe in that continuity. Because you've got to set a limit on all species. Each has its origin, its life span, its deterioration, its extinction. Do I have to tell you that mankind is just another species?"

She said, "Cast in the image of God."

"There's another statement as old-fashioned as a world with drop-off edges! Modern theologians – at least the two or three I know – would say that God is cast in the image of the ultimate of the species. If you think man is that, you've got acute astigmatism. The ultimate species on earth doesn't need a clairvoyant or a science-fiction writer to conjure him up. His grandfather's on the drawing boards of every computer company worthy of its microcircuits. If we had any tribal sense of self-preservation (which, of course, we haven't) we'd dynamite every one of those robot-planning laboratories! But we won't, so in a few generations he'll evolve off those boards – a beautiful, physically perfect plastic Adonis with a super-intelligent computer in his head-case that'll make our finest cortex look like something out of a roach. In appearance he'll be more like a man than a man, and in intelligence – yes, *real* intelligence no matter how you define it – consciousness of self, the ability to meet a new situation by proper behavior adjustments, the understanding of interrelated facts – our breed, compared to him, will be gibbering monkeys with scatterbrains and filthy habits. And those supermen will propagate their own species and limit ours to open-air zoos while they and their brethren will go out to explore the galaxies. So if God is perfection, He, too, ultimately will be beautiful and perfect and all plastic, and with an ultimate computer in His head." He grinned at her, then his smile faded. He said, "It's as inevitable as the fact that someday the sun will implode. But it's beyond our lifetimes. So take heart – and continue to believe in the Good Fairy, and the Islands of the Blessed – and, if you must, God."

Robin said softly, "I will."

Tony sighed. He said, "We're young – we should be at the new barricades. Instead we argue about a very old thing." He put out his free hand as if to touch her, then he drew it back. He said quickly, as he started the car, "Before you go see the kids, there's something at Budge Hart's I want you to see." At her hesitation he added, "I think it's important."

Robin wondered if this time she were to say no, would he finally say please. But she said, "Yes."

He shifted the gears and the car moved forward. Robin held her coat closely around herself against the cold; he saw the gesture and said, "As soon as the engine warms up, I'll turn on the heater."

In a short while he clicked a switch, and warm air curled up. Robin shivered violently.

Tony said, "What's the matter? Is it still blowing cold?"

She told him no, it was all right. But it was not all right. The sudden blast of warmth had reminded her of that strange first night in the Elias apartment; she thought, I won't go back there again – why should I? – the children have their parents, I'm nothing to them!

The man at her side said dourly, "I feel as though I'd been back in the lecture room today. I don't particularly like that. Talk, yes, but to pontificate as if I were really an expert – no, thank you. That's why I gave up teaching." At her quick glance: "Oh, yes, that's one of my small secrets. Another is that I'm a Coiler." At her puzzled look. "Coiler. From 'coil.' Like a compressed spring. Haven't you ever heard about us? We're one of the largest un-franchised fraternities in the world. We're not the Mittys of the world. Oh, no, we've really got it. The potentials. But we keep them carefully coiled away for a tomorrow when we'll strike out and change the world. Always tomorrow. And when our coils finally rust and disintegrate, no matter. There's always a younger Coiler to take our place. Oh, we're an immortal organization!"

The car was climbing into the hills again. Tony said, "If it were earlier and a weekend – it would take all of that! – I'd take you on a tour of some of your true believers here in Los Angeles."

"I know that there are believers," Robin told him without emotion. She did not want to talk anymore, argue or be argued at. The mew of the cat echoed suddenly within her. She hugged her coat close around herself.

"Oh, indeed!" said Tony Dumont. "But *what* they believe! That's what I'd like to show you. I remember some of them out of my broadcasts – the Hamasha Temple of Wisdom, the Pillar of Flame, the Church of the Tarot, the Total Church of the Total! God is a flame, or a pyramid, or a deck of cards! Take one of the latest – oh, there's one full of believers! The Muslims! God is Allah dedicated to the total extermination of the White Beast! Or another prime one I could take you to in Long Beach where they lie around naked and tele-transport each other to the highest peak in Tibet, where, in a cave, lies the only, only Ulti-mate Truth – guarded now, no doubt, by one of the Red Guard. And if that's too esoteric a handful, we could go to any of the

established believers and listen to them! 'Ah, beautiful death
with Jesus,' they chant. Yet they plead for one more breath when
their time comes to die! 'Ah, we'll meet joyously in Heaven!'
they sing. Yet every one of them weeps bitterly at the graveside!"
He stopped and grinned sheepishly, "I'm up on the dais again!"

The blind man greeted Tony's door knock with familiar truculence, then, after identifications, with obvious pleasure that
Robin had come back.

Inside the circular room, Tony said abruptly, "Budge, how
about letting me show Robin the mural?"

Robin saw the blind man's quick frown. She thought, no,
whatever it is, *no!*

"Why would she want to see that?" Budge Hart asked.

"It's a long story," Tony said.

"I've got time," the other man told him.

As Tony explained, without detail, their meeting at the
Elias home, about the prize-winning small boy, the subsequent
tragedies in the family, Robin felt distant, detached, as if all this
were about people in one of Tony's long-gone broadcasts. The
murmur of his voice was making her heavy-eyed; she wanted to
lie back, pull a curtain down over the day, and sleep – dreamless,
uninvolved sleep.

But escape was impossible; his voice went on and on, sketch-
ing the dead mother's involvement in the negative family history, and ending with their visit that afternoon to the old house
and Dave Elias's devil aberration.

"Of what benefit would it be to expose her to the mural?" the
blind man questioned.

"I told you. She's an innocent. Completely! She believes in a
haloed God on a white throne and a horned Satan on a red one."

"Why change that?"

"Really!" said Tony, getting to his feet, "I thought you, of all
people, would be of some help! I told you! She's an innocent in
our jungle! She still believes that God's watching over her from
heaven ready to swoop down angels to her rescue. She's ripe
for the first religion racketeer who comes along! Maybe your
mural will shock her into reality. She'd see how ridiculous the

demons are, that just as they are man-made, so are the angels!"
He turned to Robin. "The other night I told you there was a
law of averages that would eventually catch up with you if you
continued to walk with your eyes closed. I want you to open
them now!"

Robin had been sitting very still, hands in her lap. She said
wearily, "You constantly appear to think I'm in some sort of
danger. I don't think so. Perhaps I am naïve. But I happen to believe that there is inherent good in everyone."

He said sharply, "In Mr. Robert Farrell?"

She said, "I don't think he's really an evil man. Ambitious, yes.
Born poor and afraid to go back into poverty, yes."

Tony said, "Oh, come on now, what do you recommend,
that everyone who's poor and ambitious make pornographic
pictures? Don't you know how lucky you've been? All pink and
white and luscious, you've walked through the forest while
all the beasts were out to lunch – and when you met one, the
Marines happened to be in the neighborhood!" He turned to
the older man, who had been listening attentively. "Budge, do
you know what I mean? Every once in a while someone like her
comes along, the Innocent, eyes fixed on heaven and stepping
over the snakes and never seeing them, moving from one miracle
of escape to another without even knowing of the danger. But
sooner or later she'll meet the tiger, and she'll cry to the heaven
that isn't there, and the tiger will chew her up bit by bit and
enjoy the salty taste of her tears!"

Budge Hart smiled. He said, "You sound as if you were discussing the history of our nation." He got to his feet. He said,
"Frankly, I can't decide whether you're sincere or fighting back
an urge to rape the child."

Tony said, "Now look here – "

"So," the older man went on, "I'll stay confused and show
her the mural and we'll go on from there. Come along, my dear.
We'll keep the tiger way behind us."

Mary Elias stood by the range. She pressed the light button
and the interior of the oven lit up. A few more minutes and the
roast would be done. She looked at the wall clock. She'd serve

dinner very soon. She turned and went to the sink. She took a
glass, turned the faucet, and waited until the water was cold. She
filled the glass, turned off the rush of water, then held the glass
to her forehead. It felt good. Perhaps if she took another aspirin
. . . No, she'd taken so many, these past few days. And yet the
ache was there. And no wonder . . .

She suddenly remembered her mother's cure for an aching
head, an old Scottish prescription – horse-radish held tightly in
the hand and the headache will go. Well, why not?

She turned toward the refrigerator, then stopped. She looked
down at the glass still in her hand and drank deeply. In the madness of these past few days, was she losing her own mind? No,
she must keep her wits. God made no guarantees, her father used
to say, that one's life would be a merry-go-round of happiness.

"Mama."

She turned. Shirley. "Yes, dear?"

"Can I have a glass of water, please?"

"Of course."

She took a clean glass out of the cupboard, walked to the
sink, and filled it.

"Thank you, Mama."

"Aren't you going to drink it here?"

The small girl turned back. "It's for Mark. He's very thirsty."

"All right." She watched the little girl leave, then she sat
down wearily on one of the high-back stools. She thought,
Sam's dozing – if only I could lie down for a minute, but I don't
dare. I've remembered my dream last night – I was so small, no
older than Shirley, my mother was there, I told her I wanted to
become a nun, and she told me I'd be the bride of Jesus, and
all at once I was in a nun's long habit, and a door opened, and
Jesus came in, but he wasn't Jesus, he was a naked man, and he
walked toward my bed, and his eyes were glistening red, the way
I thought Mark's – no! Got to stop thinking! Keep busy, very
busy! Until Saturday. Blessed Saturday! She quickly got to her
feet and clenched her jaw muscles and went back to the stove
and opened the oven door. As she put on a glove and reached
for the hot rack, she stopped, turned. That high, singing sound
from Mark's room again. It added to the ache in her head. She

had spoken to him sharply about it only a little while before. He had looked at her solemnly and said, "I won't do it after tonight, Mama."

Thank God for that!

Robin Shepherd was physically ill. She had vomited and vomited, and now she was upstairs again, lying down, a cold wet cloth on her forehead, with Tony Dumont nearby cursing himself in a steady stream of invectives.

"Will you shut up?" Budge Hart exploded. "There's a bottle in the usual place, take a drink, take two, but shut up!"

After Tony had stumbled off, the blind man turned to Robin. He said, "Better?"

She nodded, then remembered and said, "Yes."

"Just lie still for a while. Close your eyes."

But when she closed her eyes, Robin saw them again, the thousands of them, as they writhed around the wall. They were gigantic beaked things and hooded things, some with the cold, merciless eyes of great snakes, others with the multifaceted look of enormous flesh-tearing mantises.

Toad-lipped and wet-eyed, flame-red and lizard-green, furred and leprous-skinned with bleeding caverns of hungry mouths, they filled the wall, ceiling to floor, circling the room in a surging nightmare.

She had followed the old man down the stairs; a click of switch and there it was, wall to wall; at first it had been only a great blur of color, a flowing madness of garish, vulgar purples and greens and reds. But as she moved closer, her heart began to race, and her face began to flame, and the heat of horror dried her lips, her mouth, as if she herself stood in the lurid-colored maelstrom.

For now she saw them clearly, the demons, the busy demons, all of them busy, holding and ripping and tearing in a vortex of intertwined bodies. Men fought in the demonic clutches – women screamed in soundless agony – children ran shrieking before the barbarous pursuit.

A curve of the wall, and she saw new monsters, great scabrous-winged creatures gleefully crushing a writhing, beseeching mass of human nakedness beneath the weight of gigantic, blood-stained talons.

Another faltering step and other demons were there in a flame-red bacchanal, claws pulling apart gleaming white thighs as others, with huge dripping members held in taloned hand, thrust madly into gasping mouths, into cringing buttocks, into shadowed, tortured clefts.

Robin wanted to turn away, close her eyes, but her legs stumbled her on and her eyes stayed open, and suddenly a new demon swam before her. He was huge, crouched, sweat glistening on red-pocked skin, towers of muscular legs firm-planted. In his arms was a child, a small, beautiful child – and Robin's tormented eyes saw that the baby's tiny arms and fingers were rigid in agony as the great Evil pressed the small body down upon its monstrous, crimson, lacerating erection.

And when she tore her eyes upward from that corruption, Robin saw that the baby's face was only half a face, that the rest of it hung from the fiend's great leering mouth.

Nausea lifted in her, then she fell into blessed darkness.

Chapter 12

Later, when she sat ashen-faced, drained – with Tony nearby dourly looking into his glass – Budge Hart said, "Permit me to say one thing. That mural is not my doing."

Tony looked up. "I always thought it was!"

"No, it isn't. This house was built by a Hollywood inventor, back in the Mary Pickford days, who was stupid enough to think that motion pictures should talk. Of course for such stupidity he got the proper response from the Hollywood moguls – 'Go away, we're doing fine, we don't need anything new, don't bother us.' After about ten years of rejection the inventor, to put it delicately, began to show certain signs of mental strain. The rumor has it that he commissioned the mural in order to evoke the devil and make an arrangement to definitely consign all motion picture executives to Hell. I doubt if he ever consummated the deal, but when he died quite naturally at a very old age and I bought the house, that door there was nailed shut with huge spikes. I finally got it open and went down the same stairs you and I just traveled. I remember I came up to the mural, opened my mouth, and suddenly I heard myself scream, 'Exorciso te immunde Spiritus!'"

Tony said, "What was that?"

"I was exorcising the devils. In my revulsion I dredged the words up 'I exorcise thee, thou unclean Spirit!' from the days when I stayed at a Catholic mission in Uganda. The old priest there did a big business in exorcisms." He smiled. "As you saw, it didn't work on paintings." He looked back at Robin with his sightless eyes. "Yes, one mural, artist unknown."

"But a very human one!" Tony stated. "You can be certain of that, eh, Budge?"

"Don't accuse me of certainty," the old man exclaimed. "During my painting years I quickly saw that certainty changed every millisecond." His head turned toward the girl. "The spinning sun was a magician playing with light beams and the moon was its apprentice. Blink your eyes and the blue of the wave is green. Hold them shut for more than a moment and the young flower has aged."

Tony said, "That's begging the question!"

"Is it really?" Budge demanded. "What certainties have you? That you exist? You're a fantasy in something's dream world! You're a three-dimensional tape running through a robot! You're a mirror image of someone in negative matter? Don't ask me to see certainties, my friend. I lost that illusion with my retinas."

Robin said softly, "Is God really dead?"

The blind man was very still for a little while, then he said, "No. God is not dead. He is in a state of metamorphosis, changing as man changes." A crow cawed beyond the walls. "When our concepts were small, He was small. A little man who walked on Earth and died in crucifixion as other men had died. But now we know our Earth is only a tiny mote in a greatness – and God has grown with that greatness until He is larger than our planet, our galaxy, our profoundest imagination."

"Mr. Elias said He was blinded," she told him. She saw his quick frown; she added, "By the fires of the Nazi crematoriums. By our atom bomb explosives."

The blind man sighed. "Perhaps. But God does not need eyes. . . ."

"Mr. Elias said He has left the world," she told him.

"For a little while, perhaps."

"But He will return?"

"Yes." He spoke gently. "He will come back someday on the great curve of space. And if, by then, we have blackened His Earth, He will weep – for the blind can weep. And under His tears the Earth will grow sweet and green once more. . . ."

Shirley Elias sprawled on the bed, the white of her slip a flower on the deep blue of the spread.

"Close your legs," Mark said without turning his head, his ear close to the loudspeaker.

She giggled but maintained her position. She said lazily, "Do I have to get all dressed up for tonight?"

"Of course!" he told her. "Absolutely!"

She turned over and lifted herself on her elbows so that she could see him. Tiny beads of sweat were on his forehead; they glistened like minute marbles. She turned over on her back again and flung her legs wide. Like Grandma. She giggled softly.

They were riding over the hills, Tony silent, grim-faced.

"I want to see the children," she had told him. "I want to make sure they're all right."

He had not argued with her; now they were headed over the canyon again toward the ocean. It was colder than it had been earlier; Robin huddled in herself and watched the headlights pull the road beneath them. The blind man's words had freshened her; after she had seen the children, she knew she would sleep well.

When they reached the top of the pass, suddenly there was a brightening on the horizon and Tony pulled the car over to the shoulder of the road. In the cup of the misted valley below a few lights gleamed like earthbound stars. Robin wondered why they had stopped. When she looked at Tony, she saw that the muscles at the side of his jaws were bunched; he suddenly said, "I'm in love with you."

The words were so unexpected that Robin was not quite sure

she had heard them, yet a faint echo of them hung between them.

"Do you know what I said to her that night?" he went on. "I said, 'I want you to be sure. Absolutely sure!'"

Robin sat unmoving; again uneasiness moved in her like a cold, strange hand.

He repeated, "'Absolutely sure.' She told me she was very sure.

"'How can you be sure?' I said.

"She said, 'I know.'

"I began to argue with her. I said, 'How can you know? I've kept you under glass.'

"She laughed and shook her head that I was wrong.

"I said, 'Okay. And some cold night, while I sit by the fire polishing my new bifocals, you'll look up from your needlepoint and you'll think, I haven't lived!'

"She said, 'Are you trying to get rid of me, Mr. Dumont?'

"I said, 'I'm trying to balance the scales. In those Army years I dated a hundred girls.'

"She laughed again.

"I said, 'You're an innocent!'" For the first time he looked at Robin. "Familiar words. Now you know why they came so easily to me. I told her, 'How can you *know*? He's a very nice guy. Okay. So tell him you'll go with him Friday night. I ask you to. I insist on it!'

"She gave me a long look. She said, 'I think you really mean that.'

"I said, 'I do! I do!'

"She went out with him that Friday. I sat there with a clock on the table. I sat there. I watched the clock. Just about now he was picking her up. I'd met him. A nice guy. Geology department at the college. Thin, distinguished-looking, good family, always in brown. He'd end up as head of his department as soon as he put on some years and got to know enough trustees. Quarter of eight. Now they must have reached the restaurant. Intimate place. A perfectly ordered dinner. The right wines. Now she was listening to him as he made dinner conversation, listening and comparing. That was good, that was fine, that was what I wanted her to do. Only me since first year in high school. Would do her good to hear another man over the candlelight. The clock said nine-thirty. Dinner was certainly over. Leaving the restaurant. The evening's young. Shall we go somewhere and dance? And she'd say, 'All right.' Hadn't I told her to? Where could they go dancing? Nightclub? Hotel? Fine, fine, either one, she'd enjoy herself. Eleven. Now she'd say, 'I think we'd better go.' I'd asked her to be back with me at midnight. 'Cinderella's hour?' she'd smiled. The clock said midnight. I listened for an auto pulling to the curb. But nothing. I went to the window. The street a tomb. When I came back to the clock, it stood at one. Where was she? Where had they gone after dancing? His place? All right, all right, wasn't that what I'd wanted? Wasn't that what I'd *really* wanted? I got a bottle. I poured a drink, another. Then another. Eileen. In another man's arms. . . . What the hell difference did it make? I'd been with other men's girls! Had my being with them wrecked them, ruined them, left them less – or more? My guts began to burn. Eileen. She hadn't wanted to go. I was drunk now. Quite drunk. Inside of his door he'd pull her close to him. His hands, those small brown hands, would begin to move. At first she'd pull away and then she'd think, it's Tony, why, of course it's Tony, always Tony! Her clothes falling to the floor, and he'd lift her, my rose-and-white Eileen, and carry her to the bed and spread her. . . . I tried to get through to the school to find out where he lived. Switchboard closed. At dawn, weeping drunk, I heard her name! An all-night radio disc jockey saying her name! I tore the phone apart calling the station! At last I had them! Eileen who? Yes, yes, they'd check the teletype. Yes, there it was. On Route 75, just before ten o'clock, a bridge had collapsed. An hour ago they pulled the car out of the river, identified the victims. *Victims!* . . . But there was more, much more that turned my life for years into a blurred nightmare. *Why* had I really done it? The pretense of balancing the scales, comparisons? No. I *knew!* My own stiff prick the answer! The crawling thoughts the answer! When she'd return, at midnight, to lift her in my arms, cover the used smeared mouth with mine, lay her on my bed, lift her smallness and thrust deep where he had been, that was what I'd really wanted, *that!*"

A night wind whispered through the tiny opening of the window next to her. Robin thought, what can I say to him? I will say nothing, see the children, then go home to blessed sleep. . . .

Tony Dumont started the car again. They moved back on the down-curving road. He said softly, without looking at her, "Was that why I took you there tonight to see that monstrosity? Oh, Robin, Robin!" His hands groped for hers. "Help me!"

She closed her hand on his. Of course she would help him. How she did not know – that was for tomorrow. But he wanted her help, and he would have it. But, first, the children. . . .

Sam Elias's gray face reflected his surprise when he opened the door and saw them standing there. He said softly, politely, "Come in. Please come in."

When they had entered the great-windowed inner room, he said, "Won't you please sit down?" He called out. "Mary, would you come in, please." He turned back to his visitors and said quickly, "You know, we've had a couple of tragedies since you were last here."

Tony murmured condolences, and Robin echoed what he said.

Mary Elias came into the room; Robin saw the tear-washed look in her face that she had seen in Sam Elias's.

Sam said, "You remember these people, Mary."

Mary Elias said, "Yes, I do," as her hands quickly undid her apron. She crumpled the cloth into a ball and stood there holding it. "How nice of you to come and see us."

Robin waited until Tony had repeated his condolences; then she said, "Are the children here?"

Father and mother looked quickly at each other. Sam Elias said, "Yeah, sure, but we don't like to bother them at a time like this."

Mary Elias added quickly, "You understand, children take family troubles very seriously. We're leaving them out of it as much as we can."

Tony said, "Of course we understand." He turned to the father. "Is your brother here yet? We met him this afternoon. He told us he was coming over."

Sam said, "No. We've been expecting him."

Mary Elias said, "Would you like some coffee? Tea?"

Tony said "No," and when the woman turned to her, Robin said carefully, "I would like to speak to Mark. Just for a moment, please."

She saw that Tony Dumont was puzzled and a shade disturbed at her persistence in seeing the boy.

Sam Elias said, "Well – " but Mary Elias interrupted with, "If I might ask, why do you want to see him? About the article you're writing?"

Robin Shepherd lied willfully for the second time in her life. She said, "Yes."

"Well, I can't see any harm in that. I'll get him." She left the room.

Sam said, "You know how it is, when you've just gone through what we have, sometimes you forget that life has to go on, especially for the kids."

Mary Elias came back into the room almost at once, trailed by the children.

"Hello, Miss Shepherd," the boy said as Shirley ran up to Mary and grasped her arm smilingly. He turned to Tony. "Good evening, sir."

Tony said, "Hi," but Robin said nothing. She watched as the boy took a seat on a chair opposite her with Shirley joining him by pulling up a footstool.

"Well, Mark," Sam Elias said loudly, "Miss Shepherd has a few more questions to ask so she can finish her article. Go ahead, Miss Shepherd."

Robin saw Mark's large eyes move to her, fix on her. She thought, what shall I say? What do I want to say? Tell him that God is not dead. He is all right, Shirley is all right, they are safely with their father and their mother. Why am I so foolish, meddling in a world that is not mine?

Tony Dumont spoke up. "Mark, is it true that you've invented a new kind of apparatus?"

Robin watched the large eyes find a new target. She thought, I'll speak to him another day. I want to leave now.

"Yes, sir," the boy said. "Would you like to hear it?"

"Not that tape-recorder again!" Sam Elias exclaimed.

Suddenly Robin felt a breath of warmth pass over her. She thought, oh, no! I'm not going to be ill again!

Mary Elias said, "I wonder where Dave is?" She spoke to Tony. "Did he say he was coming right over?"

Tony told her that was true; Robin saw Shirley look up at her brother and smile.

Again she felt the movement of warm air; she looked at the others, but there was no indication that any of them felt it, or if they did, were as disturbed by it as she was.

The boy turned to his father. He said, "Papa, please, can I play my recorder for Mr. Dumont?"

Sam Elias said sharply, "No!"

Mary Elias said, "Mark, please, don't aggravate your father."

"But I'll do it in the bedroom," the boy pleaded. "You won't even hear it. It's music, honestly!"

Sam Elias gave up. "All right, all right, but no tricks, understand?"

"Yes, Papa." He got to his feet. He said, "Do you want to hear it, Mr. Dumont?"

Tony was on his feet. He said, "Robin?"

She shook her head. The warm air was crawling. . . .

Tony said, "Okay," and followed the boy out of the room.

As Shirley started to get up, Mary Elias said sharply, "Shirley, you stay here!"

Shirley reseated herself. She said beatifically, "Yes, Mama."

Mary Elias said to Robin, "Are you sure you wouldn't like a nice drink?"

Robin managed to say, "No, thank you." She wondered if she could ask them to open a window. But even as she had that thought, the warmth was gone. She said to herself, as soon as Tony comes back, I'll ask to go. Did he really say he loved me? Or was I recalling Howard once again? I'm not quite sure – my head is muddled. Get some sleep – tomorrow I'll start functioning again. . . .

Chapter 13

Sam Elias looked at his wife. "You'd think he'd call. Dave."

Mary Elias said, "I know." She got up and walked toward the window. "Such a fog. Can't see a thing."

Sam Elias addressed Robin. "Did you have much trouble driving here?"

Robin told him that Tony had done the driving; Sam turned toward his wife by the window. "Did you hear that? When the weather is bad, she lets the man do the driving!" He turned back toward Robin. "The minute there's a little rain or something, she's got to take the wheel."

Mary Elias said, "I hope Dave didn't have trouble. That old car."

Suddenly, unexpectedly, there was music, faint, beautiful.

Sam Elias said, "How do you like that!" He turned pleasedly to his wife who had turned and was listening. "He's playing good music for a change."

Robin was listening intently; it was music such as she had never heard before. The arrangement was a complex one; she thought – she wasn't quite sure – that there were violins, and cellos, and muted woodwinds, but the combination was a strange one. Yet the music itself was – again she thought the word – beautiful. There was no other adjective for it. Faint as it was, coming through the closed door down the hall, it permeated the room like a perfume, drifting around her on the warmth, back again, now, but pleasant, very pleasant.

Sam got to his feet. He said, "Now that's more like it! This I'm perfectly willing to listen to! I'll get him to bring it in." He started out of the room.

Mary Elias said, "Sam!"

He turned to her.

She said, "Do you think it's proper – "

Sam said, "Why not? Good music isn't disrespectful."

She nodded, and he turned and left the room.

Robin saw that Shirley was beaming happily; Mary Elias sat back on the couch and said, "You never know about that boy." She addressed her smiling daughter. "You like it?"

Shirley nodded vigorously.

"I don't blame you. It is very lovely." She addressed Robin. "He must have re-recorded it off one of those high-fidelity FM stations. Have I heard it before? Or did I hear it on the Muzak thing in the elevator?" She shrugged. "Me with music! I'm still a bagpipe girl." She smiled at Robin. "I'm of Scottish ancestry."

Sam Elias reentered the room. He was carrying the tape-recorder with Tony carrying the smaller equipment, followed by the boy.

"Well, here we are," Sam said. "For everybody to enjoy."

Robin suddenly felt a pinpoint of high heat beaming down on her; she looked up, startled.

But there was nothing above her; only the crystal chandelier in the center of the ceiling; even as she looked the concentration of warmth faded and was gone.

As the father helped the boy connect the apparatus, Tony came over to Robin. He said, "That's really high fidelity. Did you hear it?"

Robin did not answer. She thought. I'll tell him now about the heat, that I want to leave. But he went right on speaking.

"I don't see how he gets that frequency range out of such a small loudspeaker," he said. "He gets as much quality out of that little thing as we get back at the station out of our huge monitor speakers."

Sam Elias announced, "He said it's ready!"

Mary Elias said, "Shouldn't we wait until Dave gets here?"

Sam took a seat beside her. He said, "To listen to good music?" He waved a dismissing hand. "Go ahead, Mark. Turn it on."

Robin thought, as long as it doesn't grow warm again, I'll wait. Another few minutes. Just a few . . .

"Yes, Papa." The boy pressed a switch and Robin saw the tapes begin to revolve. Music began to drift through the loudspeaker, lovely at first, the melodic strain that she had heard before. Then slowly, subtly, it changed in mood. The harmony ended; harp arpeggios began; a flute called. Or was it a flute? Strange notes lifted, plucked untuned steel strings sounded, a woodwind cried out like a creature lost in darkness.

Sam said, "Hey, that's getting modern!"

Mary Elias nodded.

Robin felt the hairs on her arms moving like tiny insects. She wanted to rise, but her legs would not move; her toes scuffed aimlessly at the carpet.

Mary Elias said, "Very, very modern."

Shirley grinned.

The music was now a beehive of dissonance – tuneless, unknown instruments in a busy cacophony of tonal conversation.

Suddenly it was there again, the warmth; Robin looked toward Tony; she saw that he was sitting tensely erect; yes, he, too, must be experiencing that swirl of heat. In a moment he would turn to her and say, "Come on! Let's go! Get out of here!"

Again the music changed; abruptly it was molten metal, sparks rising, pouring in a crimson waterfall over glowing rocks, great clouds of writhing steam uplifting. . . .

Robin thought, hurry, Tony, hurry, say it! Please! I'm getting dizzy! I've got to close my eyes!

Sam Elias said, "Well, I guess that's about enough. Turn it off, Mark! Did you hear me? I told you to – "

He stopped as a voice began far behind the music, a cracked old voice, singing without words in vague counterpoint to the swirl of dissonance.

Robin's eyelids came open. She saw that the faces of both Sam and Mary Elias were suddenly bloodless; they were seated ramrod straight, their eyes on the shadowed grille of the loudspeaker.

After a long moment Sam Elias turned his head slowly toward his son. He said in a strangulated voice, "Are you doing it again?"

The boy said quietly, "Doing what, Papa?"

Sam Elias's voice climbed. "You know damn well what! It's *her* voice! You taped *her* voice!"

Mary Elias said, "Oh, Mark, Mark!"

The singing stopped abruptly, and then the music stopped, and as Robin thought, I'm grateful, the harsh voice spoke through the loudspeaker. It said, "Hello, Sam. Hello, Mary."

Sam Elias shook his head dazedly, like a fighter clearing his head after a punch. He looked at his son. He said, "Why?" His voice rose as he got to his feet. *"Why? Answer me!"*

He moved toward the boy, but with a quick movement Mary Elias stood between him and her son. She was breathing heavily. She said, "Let him alone! Is he to blame for what she made him do?"

The old voice through the loudspeaker mocked: "Blame for what she made him do?"

Tony Dumont saw the mother and father freeze where they stood. He looked at their stricken faces and he thought, what the hell is going on here? He looked over at Robin Shepherd. He saw that her forehead was beaded with sweat. He thought, I don't get this! What is it? What should I do?

Robin Shepherd thought, if I throw something at the window, break it, the air will rush in and I'll be able to breathe again. Words began to scream in her head. *I'm ill, I'm very ill, I've got to get out of here!* She turned to Tony. She gasped, "Tony – " but his attention was focused on the equipment; she knew he heard her because he put up a hand without looking at her, as if to say, "Later! Later!"

Tony thought, this is plain stupid! I'm in a luxury apartment in a steel-concrete building in Westwood Village, California, I'm an educated man, I could have had my master's in another six months, I've got a top-rated radio show, CBS has been talking a deal with me, a million people listen to me every week, I know all the answers, what in hell am I doing here listening to this crap in this crazy family? The kid doctored the tape, this smart-ass kid, I've doctored tape, you put the tape in the machine, you pull it back and forth over the playback head until you get the words you want, you mark the place, the beginning, the end, you put it in the splicer, you cut it out, you lay in the other words you need, you butt the cut ends together, you slap on a piece of mending tape, and there, you've got it made! That's what the kid did! There's no supernatural – nothing but a smart-ass kid and his electronic trickery!

Sam Elias found his voice. He grated, "Why did she tell you to play it to us tonight?"

The brittle old voice crawled out of the loudspeaker again. "I didn't make him do it, Sam."

Tony saw horror wash out the humanity in the listening faces. He thought, that voice is talking in the present! *In the present!*

The old woman's voice went on: "He's my bright boy – how many times do I have to tell you? They're both of them mine!"

Mary Elias turned tortured eyes toward her husband. "It isn't true! It isn't! She's not talking! Pre-recorded!"

Robin Shepherd struggled to her feet. She stood there swaying. The room was red, everyone red. She thought, I can't stand another moment of this heat, I'm burning, I'm on fire! She turned and staggered out of the room.

Only the children's eyes watched her go. The others were intent on the grilled speaker as the voice went on: "It's lonely where I am. I like people with me. The others are with me. Why shouldn't you be?"

Tony Dumont thought, this is fantastic! The boy has anticipated every reaction, put together old recordings to scare the hell out of his father and mother! What a macabre trick!

The voice went on. "He's with me, too, now, Sam. He went over a cliff into the sea a little while ago. Wasn't that thoughtful of your brother David?"

Sam Elias swayed like a tree struck by a savage burst of wind. He did not turn as Mary Elias, slowly, slowly, sank to her knees.

Tony Dumont felt a strange tightness in his chest. He thought, Dave Elias? How could the boy have known *that*? He began to get to his feet slowly, slowly, his eyes tight on the whirling reel feeding the tiny loudspeaker.

The old voice went on without pity: "When I was with you, Dave never did amuse me. Neither did Nat. Neither did Harriet. They don't now. Come amuse me, Sam. You and Mary. Take her hand, Sam. Take it. *Take it!*"

Tony Dumont watched in growing horror as the man's hand went into the woman's.

"Lift her up, Sam. *Now!*"

The strong hand in hers lifted the woman from her knees.

"Now go toward the window. You and Mary. Hand in hand. Go, Sam! Mind your mother!"

Tony Dumont gasped for breath. The constriction in his chest was worse, much worse. But he couldn't tear his eyes away from the man and the woman walking stiff-legged toward the window, toward the infinity beyond.

"Another step, Sam. Now another. And another. Open the terrace door."

Sam's free hand turned the knob. Traffic sounds filtered upward.

"Another step, Sam. Mind your mother. Now walk, Sam. Walk and walk and – "

Mary Elias shrieked, "No!" She tore her hand loose, turned, rushed to the apparatus, picked up a chair, swung it high, and crashed it down on the mechanism. The loudspeaker crushed, and the old voice stopped, and a reel leaped off the falling recorder and spun madly across the floor leaving a long snake of brown tape behind it.

Tony Dumont stood in the sudden silence. He could hear Mary Elias weeping heavily into her hands and Sam's broken voice as he moved close and held her. "It's all right, Mary. It's all right. . . ."

"You're damn right, it's all right!" Tony cried out. "It was a trick, a magician's trick! He's not a genius, that son of yours! He's a psychotic little madman! Put him away!"

He felt sudden heat and he spun around. Fire! The broken apparatus was burning on the floor! As he turned and ran toward the telephone, he heard a tremendous crackling sound behind him, and, when he turned again, he saw that the small flame was a great flame, rising quickly, fantastically growing, red beyond red, the roar increasing so that he vaguely heard the screams behind him.

He felt the heat scorching him; he threw the telephone from him and ran toward the outer door, but a ceiling-high section of the flame suddenly curved downward like a great, taloned hand and covered the entry.

He thought, the children, get the children! But when he turned, he could not see the children because the flame had turned white, incandescent, like a great staring eye, and Mary Elias was in the midst of it, clawing, fighting, and suddenly his own eyes could see no more.

He shrieked, "Oh, God, please! *Please!*" but the words were only in his head, and they were lost in the searing flesh.

When she left the Elias building, Robin stood outside and gratefully sucked in the cooling air. After a moment she saw that a cab was at the curb and that the driver was staring puzzledly at her. She walked to the car, opened the door, and got in.

The cabman said, "Are you all right, lady?"

She did not answer him. She gave her address. She sat rigidly, her eyes closed.

During the short ride, the taximan kept looking in his rear-vision mirror. He wondered if this pretty young chick was high on something. He speeded up. Get rid of her fast as possible.

When the cab got to her apartment house, Robin found that she did not have her purse. She whispered to the cab-driver that she had to get money upstairs. He grunted skeptically and followed her up to her apartment and waited outside until she brought him the cash. She walked slowly back into her apartment and closed the door. She went to her bed and lay down in it. She closed her eyes.

She awoke with a start to the sound of distant sirens. They were rising and falling, a multiplicity of them. She sat listening a moment, then her hand went out and she turned on the small transistor set next to her bed.

"Fantastic fire!" The announcer's voice was supercharged with excitement. "The entire circular building is wrapped in flames. A thirty-story funeral pyre!"

Robin Shepherd threw herself from the bed. She rushed out of the apartment, the door remaining open behind her. She ran down the stairs, half-falling, grasping at the railing. In the street she threw herself into her automobile still parked curbside at the entrance. She found she had no purse, no key. She groped under the dashboard until her fingers closed on the magnetic-backed container that carried the emergency key. She threw the cover aside and grasped the key and put it into the ignition switch. Her fingers twisted; the motor caught, roared; her hand yanked down on the shift lever and the small car tore away from the curb, tires squealing.

Long before she reached Wilshire Boulevard she could hear the scream of fire apparatus moving down the thoroughfare. She was weeping now, uncontrollably, as she turned up a parallel street and steered the automobile toward the great glow on the western sky.

More and more automobiles were paralleling her. At last she could go no further and she opened the door of the car and ran from it down street after street until finally, pushing and clawing, she was through to the final police barrier. It was ahead, the fire; she lifted tear-filled eyes and saw that the flame was all, there was no building, only the flame.

She found new tears, but even as she wept them, the great heat lifted them from her face.

Suddenly there were small hands in hers, on either side of her! She looked down. The children! The blessed children! She hugged them to her and their little arms were about her and she thought, oh, I am blessed! I will have the children! To care for and to love! Forever I will teach them kindness and goodness and wash away this horror with my love, all my love!

Their small trusting hands in hers, she led them away from the fire, but she could not stop weeping at the miracle of it. The blessed, blessed children!

As they walked along, Shirley smiled happily at her brother across the movement of Robin Shepherd's dress.

The small boy skipped and ran a step to keep up with the woman who was holding his hand so tightly. He looked up at her. The air, moving past them toward the vortex of fire, was molding her skirt to her body, blowing her dark hair away from her intent young face. He smiled covertly as he thought, Grandma is right, Miss Shepherd *is* very wide-eyed and pink and white. . . .